'So,' said Menn...
to the door. It was, Brannock thought, an insuf
ficient farewell for a king's son going on an errand
of great import; and unfeeling besides. He
mounted and looked down on Mennor, and a
terrible feeling of inadequacy came over him.

'Mennor,' he said, 'I don't think I – I'm afraid
of failing you.'

'That's the most sensible thing you've said yet,'
Mennor returned cheerfully. 'You're beginning
well. I'll give you one hint before you go. Try passing the stone circle on your left hand. And good
luck go with you.'

He actually bowed. It was not a very deep bow,
but more than Brannock had expected from him.

Also available in Beaver
by Jean Morris

The Donkey's Crusade

THE TROY GAME

Jean Morris

BEAVER BOOKS

A Beaver Book
Published by Arrow Books Limited
62–65 Chandos Place, London WC2N 4NW
An imprint of Century Hutchinson Ltd

London Melbourne Sydney Auckland
Johannesburg and agencies throughout the world

First published in 1987 by The Bodley Head
Beaver edition 1989
Copyright © Jean Morris 1987

Set in Sabon
Typeset by JH Graphics Ltd, Reading

Made and printed in Great Britain
by Courier International Ltd
Tiptree, Essex

ISBN 0 09 962080 4

To my daughter Mercy,
who first showed me the
pattern of the troy

One

The children were waiting outside the king's hall, and as Brannock came up the village street they made for him, shouting that they needed his help. He waved them away, but two of the boys hooked his arms and hung on, saying, 'Do come, Brannock, we've lost our best ball, and you're the only one who can find it.'

He tried to shake them off, saying with what he hoped was dignity, 'I am summoned to the king my father;' but that only made them laugh.

'Never mind about him; you never do mind anyway. It's gone into the brambles somewhere in that old troy, and you know you can find anything.'

One of the girls said primly, 'It's their own fault it's lost, playing ball in the troy. You always lose things if you do that.'

All the boys said at once, 'Nonsense. No one believes those old stories now. Girls always spoil a good game. Come along, Brannock, take no notice of them.'

'Not even Brannock will find it in the troy,' said another girl.

'Oh yes, he will. Do be quick, Brannock, and show her she's wrong.'

'Yes,' a new voice said, 'prove her wrong, Brannock, if you can.' And they all stopped and fidgeted, even Brannock, because their village elder,

7

Mennor, was standing in the door of the hall watching them.

It was childish, they knew, to believe that Mennor could appear and disappear at will. But for such a big man, broad-chested and long-striding in spite of his grey beard, he was able to make his way remarkably quietly to places where he was not expected, or even welcomed; very little went on that stayed hidden from him. Brannock, who had been allowing the boys to drag him away, stopped at once.

'No,' Mennor said to him, 'why shouldn't you show off your trick?' He said *trick* with a very sharp look. 'Where did they say the ball was lost?'

The boys led the way in a noisy procession, and Brannock, not very willingly, went with them. The girls, who like all girls were much less frightened than they made out, clustered round Mennor and said in their self-righteous way, 'But it is so, isn't it, Mennor? They shouldn't play in the troy, should they? And you never do find things when they've been lost there.'

Mennor said, striding along without appearing to take much notice of them, 'Even the women have forgotten the secrets of the troy.'

This started an argument among the girls, who did not like to admit that they had forgotten any of the old charms, even though the troy game was never done now because no one knew exactly how it should go; but by that time they had arrived at the level circle of turf where the troy had once been cut. Under the scutch only the faintest outline of the old pattern could be seen, the seven circles, each only wide enough for a foot; the smallest circle in the centre had disappeared altogether under an arch of bramble and nettles. The boys were wrestling and leap-frogging along its edges. They were noisy in their scorn of the girls, but if one of them put a foot in the troy he took it off very quickly.

'Well then, Brannock,' said Mennor.

A little reluctantly, Brannock opened the wallet on his belt and took out his bob; at which the children said, 'That's it, that's right!' and clustered round him to watch. The bob was nothing but a thong of leather weighted by a pebble with a hole in it. He had tried other things that worked, in particular a forked twig of hazel, but he liked the bob because it was easy to carry with him. He asked, 'Does anyone remember whereabouts the ball fell?'; but no one did, so he rubbed his fingers, steadied his wrist, and let the bob swing free. It hung dead, so he stepped into the troy. The bob came alive then, not moving much but giving him the familiar tingle in his fingers. They had called the ball their best one; it would be that big one made of six pieces of leather. He pictured it in his mind, and the bob at once began to swing. He followed it to the centre of the troy.

One of the boys called, 'Not there, it went somewhere on your right.'

Brannock took no notice. The bob took him in a short bend round the brambles, and then stopped him and swung strongly towards the heart of the troy.

The boys, who knew the signs, shouted joyfully, 'Yes, in there!' Offended, he said, 'I'm not crawling into that.'

'He's afraid for his nice new tunic,' the girls said, giggling. This was true; it was a rich berry-red, and he had put it on for the first time today. Mennor said, 'Who has a good knife?', and because he did not appear to disapprove the boys went scrambling in and hacked at the brambles. The ball was lying among the

9

roots, just where the bob had indicated. They pitched it back and forth amongst them, cheering, and started to sprint away. Mennor stopped them, saying, 'Keep away from the troy in future.'

'Yes, all right, we'll remember. Thanks, Brannock. You girls coming?'

They dashed away, but the girls stayed around Mennor. 'No, Mennor, do be serious. We'd do the troy game if we knew how, but even the grandmothers who say they did it when they were young can't remember the pattern, and no one bothers to keep it clear. But it isn't a good place to play in, is it? Something always goes wrong if you do.'

Mennor said, 'If something is forgotten you can't bring it back; however valuable it was. As for this poor troy's being a place for games, it is if you feel it is, and it isn't if you feel it isn't. Now be off.'

The girls went away subdued. Brannock had been kicking away the slashed brambles, wondering if they would reveal the pattern at the centre of the troy; but the thick roots had spoilt it. He said to Mennor, 'My father sent for me. I suppose he has some errand to be done.'

'No doubt. And for me,' said Mennor, as usual knowing everything that went on, 'he has not sent. So we'll go together.'

Since the king and his elder seldom agreed, this sounded interesting. Brannock fell into step, saying with an attempt at casualness, 'Finding things is only a trick I do. I don't know how.' Mennor's watching had made him self-conscious about it.

'I didn't think you did. Do you know what else you can find?'

'Oh yes.' He had discovered the trick one year when the nut-game had been in fashion. One threaded a nut on a string and tried to smash everyone else's nut. When he had discovered that his nut sometimes came alive with the tingle in his fingers, he had spent a long time experimenting with it. 'Water; I can find water even far underground. And metal is easy; I don't even have to concentrate on metal. Stone circles and standing stones; I don't like them, they're so strong they send my bob wild. And sometimes paths; I got out of a marsh once by finding the path.'

'Why,' said Mennor, stopping at the door of the king's hall, 'did your father send for you?'

'He's had a guest overnight; sly-eyed and sour-faced, some kind of relation from east somewhere. Since you don't know about him, it must be a secret visit. He'll need putting on his way. I can be trusted with that,' said Brannock with a grin. He was the king's younger son, and very skilled in avoiding tiresome duties.

'Secret no longer,' said Mennor with unaccountable grimness, and motioned him in.

Hywel the king was talking to his sour-faced guest on the dais half-way down the long hall, and scowled to see the two of them together. 'My second boy Brannock, the village elder Mennor. My cousin Petrock; well – far-out cousin,' he introduced them. Mennor gave the visitor a bow so slight it was barely civil. Brannock sighed to have even a far-out cousin in a tunic so badly cut, and made him an elaborate salutation, adjusting his own belt to be sure his new tunic hung in the proper folds. The guest Petrock, sadly unimpressed, nodded coolly to them both and turned to the king.

'Since I know your mind, sir, I can take my leave. And if your son will—'

His meaning was so clear that Brannock had begun

11

to turn to the door; but the king interrupted in a hurry.

'I think not. No no, not you, Brannock. Conan – Conan, are you there? My elder son will see you on your way. Conan!'

'Oh?' said Petrock, cocking his head at him. He looked thoughtfully at Brannock and avoided looking at Mennor, and a faint sardonic grin spread over his face. 'By all means, by all means, cousin!'

Conan, with his usual air of sickening helpfulness, appeared from the inner rooms, and the king said to him, 'Our guest is leaving, you can ride to the ford with him. Don't hang about, boy, he's in a hurry.'

Conan, who never saw beyond the end of his nose, said blankly, 'Yes, Father, yes, sir,' and took the guest off, bleating anxiously about the readiness of horses. When they were safely gone, the king took his high seat, wriggling his shoulders into it with an unconscious sigh of relief, and said, 'Well, Mennor; did you want to see me?'

'*You* wanted to see *me*,' Brannock reminded him, irritated to have had his time wasted.

'Well, Conan was here; he can be trusted to be polite to a guest.'

Mennor said without expression, 'And to see him off before I can speak to him.'

'Brannock,' said the king, 'you can go.'

'He had better stay,' said Mennor. 'You know why I wanted to see you; we discussed it yesterday. Has anything happened to change your mind?'

'No,' said the king at once; 'certainly not. I may have had a word with Petrock about it, but he's a travelled man, his opinion's worth having. And it happens to be the same as mine. You're taking these rumours too seriously.'

12

'We disagree,' said Mennor. 'And I ask your permission to send your younger son on the errand we spoke of.'

'My permission?' the king said sourly. 'As if either of you ever took notice of what I say. Oh, send the boy if you want to, he's no use to me. And if you think you can trust him not to go idling through the land in his usual way.'

'Thank you,' said Mennor, and turned to go. His air was so serious that Brannock followed him without complaining that he had not been consulted.

'A better idea, though,' said the king, cheering up a little: 'why not go yourself? Add more weight to the message, no need to rely on the boy – much better, don't you think?'

Mennor looked at him over his shoulder and said, 'No. After the visit of your far-out cousin, I see that I shall be needed here.' And he strode out of the hall.

Outside he said briefly to Brannock, 'Fetch what you need for a journey and come to my hut. Quickly.'

Left blinking, Brannock called after him, 'For how long?'

'What you can carry,' said Mennor without stopping.

In case anyone should think him abashed by this abruptness, Brannock shrugged elaborately and went into his sleeping-place, shouting to the girls to pack him a food-bag and to one of the men to bring round his horse. Wherever the mysterious errand took him, he had no intention of appearing as anything less than the well-dressed son of a king. He combed his hair into the fashionable warrior's mane, put his torque round his neck, and carefully pinned the cloak on his shoulder with its circular gold brooch. Then he decided that his own boots were shabby and

13

rummaged until he found Conan's best pair. Conan arrived as he was pulling them on, and said smugly, 'You can borrow them if you like.'

'I have borrowed them. Do you know what's going on?'

'Well, Father's ordered his war-gear scoured, but I haven't heard of any trouble in the kingdoms, have you? They've even paid most of their tribute on time.' Hywel was at this time high king of the Seven Kingdoms (as they were called; though the smaller ones were not much bigger than a village and its few fields). Every now and again there was a squabble and a few skirmishes and someone else called himself high king for a season or two.

'Who was that cousin Petrock?'

'He wasn't a cousin,' said Conan in surprise. 'Just a traveller from the east, sleeping here overnight. I think he had a message from our uncle Rhodri.'

'Oh, the east,' said Brannock, losing interest. East of the Seven Kingdoms was nothing but waste land where it was worth no one's time to go. He grinned a little, heartlessly, to have found his father trying to deceive Mennor.

Conan came to the door of the hall with him. 'It's my opinion,' he offered, 'that what's worrying Father is these rumours about raiders from the east.'

'These rumours have been hanging around ever since I can remember,' Brannock said. Ingaret and Aeronwy, his sisters, came out arguing about what should go in the food-bag, and Conan linked hands to mount him. None of them troubled to say goodbye to him; they were used to his absences.

He trotted his horse along the street to the out-skirts, where Mennor's hut stood within sight of the stone circle on a rise a quarter of a mile away. He did

14

not like the outside of the hut, for the stone circle had an uneasy effect on him, but its inside had always fascinated him. Mennor had a mania for buried bits and pieces which other people would have kicked aside, and when they had been washed and scraped and burnished they took on, though broken and incomplete, a queer air of value.

'But *what* value?' Brannock had once asked, a small boy tagging at Mennor's heels as he prowled around old ruins and nettle-smothered ditches.

'Value to the men who were here before us,' Mennor had replied shortly. 'Do you never think about them?'

Stepping in now out of the sunlight, he complained, 'I would like to know what is this errand I am to be sent on.'

'That's what you are here for,' Mennor said sharply. But he was less decided than usual, staring out of the door at the distant stone circle, which sent out tiny sparkles from its rough grey surface. 'It's a risk,' he said, more to himself than to Brannock. 'If there were any other way I wouldn't take it; I'd go myself. But I shall be more use here; I don't trust your—' He met Brannock's lively eye and corrected himself: 'I don't trust affairs here.'

Brannock laughed to himself; he knew quite well that Mennor did not trust his father to stir himself in time of trouble. But it would not do to repeat all Conan's gossip, so he said only, and with truth, 'I'm a good traveller, and I can keep a secret.'

'I need more than that,' Mennor said sharply. 'Now don't turn haughty on me! There's far more to this errand than knowing every path in the Seven Kingdoms. I know you can do that: what your father calls idling through the land. I need you to do an

15

errand to a place to which there is no path; to go to the hall of my Order.'

'That's a fine way to send someone on an urgent errand,' Brannock said. He said it brightly, to hide his shock; and, if it had to be admitted, his moment of fright. Everyone knew that at the four divisions of the year the elders disappeared from their villages to confer together in the hall of their Order; promising young men disappeared there too, to return years later as elders themselves. But of the whereabouts of this hall no one knew more than that the elders rode away, carrying food for several days, towards the waste-lands in the east. Some said that then they rode to a bare hillside and spoke a charm that opened it for them to ride inside and have it close again after them. Most people, pointing out that only the women ever did charms these days, simply said that the hall was farther east into the waste than anyone else troubled to go.

'Did I say you would find it easy?' Mennor returned snappishly. 'Few people outside the Order have seen that hall; none in my lifetime. It is protected by a secret of the land itself.'

This was interesting. 'I'm to be the only one to go? Then you'll give me a charm so that I can get in?' Brannock suggested.

'Will you kindly *think*!' Mennor said sharply. 'I have told you that the hall is protected by the land itself. Do you really imagine that any charm I could make would be stronger than that?'

'Oh. I suppose not. Then how am I to get there?'

'By your own powers. You have the favour of the land. Use your bob.'

There was a great deal, most of it outraged, that Brannock would have said to this; but under

16

Mennor's look it died into a stutter. He said uncertainly, 'At least tell me where to start!'

Mennor for the first time smiled. 'You start where we start, at the edge of the eastern wild. If you ride now you can reach Eastmark by sundown, and sleep the night at your uncle Rhodri's hall. The elder Illtud will be there, and he will take you tomorrow morning to the spot where the charm begins; from that spot you will use your own powers. Is that understood?'

Brannock muttered that understood was not the word. 'Does Illtud know what he is to do? And what about when I get to the hall of the Order? If I ever do,' he added, but not aloud.

'I have tokens for you to deliver.'

The token for Illtud was a small written packet, which Brannock put in his wallet, but the other was a square of leather with only three runes boldly marked on it. He looked dubiously at them, for he was not skilled in runes and thought he recognized only his own B-rune in the second.

'The first is mine,' said Mennor, 'and will mark you as my messenger. The third you won't know, nor anyone else outside my Order. It names what must be done. No – not in your wallet, wallets get lost; round your neck.' He tied it into a thong, and Brannock obediently put it over his head.

'But aren't I to tell them – well, isn't there anything I am to tell them?'

'You will find that they know more about affairs in the Seven Kingdoms than you have ever known. That's part of our work.'

'Well, all right, I never did pay attention to politics. So then I don't understand why you have to tell them what to do in one rune. Why don't they know it already?'

'A little intelligence,' Mennor said detachedly, 'is always useful, but a good deal more is desirable. That rune doesn't *tell* anyone what to do, and I didn't say it did. It might have ocurred to you that one does not *tell* the Order of elders to do anything. The third rune casts my vote for the final course of action.'

'Final?' Brannock said uneasily. The word had a ring that overcame even his resentment at being not quite intelligent enough.

'Final: last and worst: so much the worst that they wouldn't venture on it without the consent of each one of the Order. I am not sending you, Brannock, on any inconsiderable errand.'

'Oh. Well. All right,' said Brannock. The assurance gave him dignity, he supposed, but did not make his errand sound any easier. He was turning to the door when Mennor called him back, opening one of his chests.

'What did you use to make your bob?'

'What? Just a pebble with a hole in it.'

'Show me.'

Brannock handed it over, saying, 'It doesn't matter what it is, you know. Just so long as it's heavy enough to swing freely.'

'You think so?' said Mennor, and rubbed his thumb round the pebble. It was a smooth yellow one with a natural hole, the kind the children collected for their rarity. He stooped to the chest and brought out one by one a variety of the odd objects that had once so fascinated Brannock. There was a blue-black flint that had somehow become a bright barbed arrow-head, point and tangs so fine that the light shone through them; a piece of worn bone in the shape of a pick, and another with scratches that might almost have been the picture of an animal, if any animal

18

could be imagined with such great humped shoulders and lowered charging head; a piece of flat stone with the remains of a flower-pattern in ochre and green; four small beads still brilliantly blue; and, best of all, two curved pieces of iridescent glass, no thicker than a dead leaf.

Handling these delicately, Brannock exclaimed, 'But look, they fit together! They're part of something—'

'They were once a drinking-cup,' said Mennor, taking them tenderly back and wrapping them in wool. 'It may be that you will see one on your journey. It was made by men who once lived in this land; all these things were. What do you think of this?'

He handed over a dull little object, an incomplete circle of metal. Looking more closely, Brannock saw that it was gold, scratched and pitted, finely incised and worked with patterns in which some traces of a red colour were still visible.

'It's a brooch,' he said enviously, for it must once have been finer than the one he wore on his shoulder.

'It was a brooch. The pin has worn away in the earth. It was made and worn by men long dead who lived and worked in this land. I think it will have value in finding out the secrets of this land. Tie it on your thong.'

Brannock had no views about its value, since a half-shattered nut had made him a serviceable bob, but he was pleased to have such a fine thing, and unknotted his pebble willingly enough. But when he had it free to toss away a curious feeling of shame came over him at the thought of discarding something he had had so long. When he put the new bob into his wallet, he slipped the pebble in with it.

'So,' said Mennor, 'you are ready,' and took him to

the door. It was, Brannock thought, an insufficient farewell for a king's son going on an errand of great import; and unfeeling besides. He mounted, settled the food-bag on his shoulder and looked down on Mennor, and a terrible feeling of inadequacy came over him.

'Mennor,' he said, 'I don't think I – I'm afraid of failing you.'

'That's the most sensible thing you've said yet,' Mennor returned cheerfully. 'You're beginning well. I'll give you one hint before you go. Try passing the stone circle on your left hand. And good luck go with you.'

He actually bowed. It was not a very deep bow, but more than Brannock had expected from him.

Two

The first thing that happened on the errand of great import was that he saw his dog racing to catch him up. He had no intention at all of taking him, because, although well-bred and handsome and all that the dog of a king's son should be, he was only a year old and could have been more obedient. Brannock should have trained him, but they had spent the time instead happily romping and rambling. He reined up and said sternly, 'Home, Goldeneye! Go home!' Goldeneye leapt joyously round him and scudded on ahead. He considered catching him and taking him back, but that would have been an anti-climax. And, after all, it was a suitable picture, the king's son on his handsome horse with his handsome dog at his side – nearly at his side. 'But if you disgrace me—!' he muttered after him.

This had brought him half-way past the stone circle, which he was passing on his right hand with the usual path. He never did go the other way, he realized. He turned his horse's head and called to Goldeneye. It did not surprise him that Goldeneye took no notice, but he was surprised that his horse at first resisted the rein and then turned skittery and had to be forced to walk this way. It was counter-sunwise, which was generally, although vaguely, regarded as the unlucky way. The stone circle itself was regarded as not so much unlucky as uneasy. The rise on which

21

it stood was very slight, but there seemed to be no spot from which you could not see it. No one quite knew why it was there, except possibly Mennor, who said nothing. Anyone could see that it was aligned on the path of the moon, and everyone knew that at times Mennor was busy there at night. Some said that he was making sure that the moon rose at the right spot, others that he was making it rise; yet others that it was all nonsense these days; but no one ever went near enough to watch him. All that Brannock knew about it was that the circle of quiet turf inside it was not so much unpleasant as *demanding*. It allowed nothing in his mind and memory but the look, the air, the smell of every spot in the land, from the little garden plot he had grubbed in as a child to the broad downs and silent forests where he preferred to spend his days now. And as for riding round it counter-sunwise – yes, it felt disagreeable, as if he were stroking fur backwards. The day seemed suddenly darker, and when he looked up at the sky there came a singing in his head and a cold sweat on his forehead. Was the stone circle turning round him – turning sunwise – or was he going to come off in a humiliating fit of faintness? And before he knew which it was the horse bolted.

It was absurd; it was outrageous. The horse was well-schooled and he was the best rider of his age. The business of keeping his seat wiped the faintness from his mind; but, to make the outrageous worse, the horse slowed of its own accord as soon as they were past the stone circle, so that he could not even tell himself that it was his own doing. He reined in and looked back to find what it was that had startled it; there must have been something, for surely going the wrong way round the circle could not make a quiet animal bolt? But there was nothing; all he could see was that he had been out of sight of the village, so that at least no one had seen his shame. Then he looked farther, and saw to his fury that there *had* been someone to see him. His mother was sitting on the threshold stone outside the entrance of the circle.

He cantered back to her with a great display of horsemanship, ready to persuade himself that a rabbit had started under his horse's feet. But all she said was, 'You will need this,' and gave him the old tunic she had on her lap. He took it sulkily; he knew she meant that in her view he should not be wearing his new tunic for a journey. Her name was Ia, and he took after her; she was a tall woman, with a great rope of waving yellow hair, and when she chose to speak out not even Mennor could stand against her. This, however, seldom happened, because she was busy about her own affairs, being learned in women's charms, and these, which were concerned with such things as the growth of seeds and the welfare of bees and beasts, the men did not worry about. Brannock had not quite grown out of asking her for help in puzzles, and said, 'Mother, do you know how my bob finds things that are lost?'

She said briskly, 'How does the sun get up or the seed grow? It's in their nature to do so.'

'Yes, but Mennor says I have to find my way by the bob.'

'Then be thankful, my son, that you don't have to find your way without it.'

He muttered, 'That's just like a woman.'

'What do you expect me to be like? You were an annoying child, Brannock, but I never had to worry that you would get lost. But let me tell you something. Mennor trusts you to carry his message because he

23

thinks you love the land as he does. I don't think you do.' Absently, her fingers were smoothing the turf at her side. 'You are the one who can work the bob, not Mennor. Your land-sense will guide you; but remember that it may not guide you to what you want. The land may have its own wants. And now – you're going to your uncle's for the night? Give my love to Iorwenna and the children, and tell her I shall keep her a crock of my clover-honey.'

She said a temperate goodbye – she was never a mother to hang lovingly over her children – and went away, sunwise past the circle. Brannock watched her bitterly. As if Mennor had not given him enough of a puzzle, she must add to it!

He reached the kingdom of Eastmark comfortably before sunset. Afer Hywel's Waymark it was the largest of the seven, but it could still be ridden across in a day. Rhodri had married Iorwenna, who was the sister of Ia of Waymark, and had come into his kingdom chiefly because there was no one else more suitable. People liked him in a tolerant way, but in trouble went to Iorwenna. He was a small shuffling man with a watery humorous eye and a love of gossip. He received Brannock with gratifying ceremony, gave him a very good supper, and sat late with him afterwards cheerfully talking scandal. About the danger from the east he nodded with great seriousness, sent someone to find Illtud, and carried on with the scandal.

Illtud came in presently, wrapped in a heavy cloak against the night air and helping a lame leg along with a stick. Elders, whose memories had to hold the history of all the kingdoms, as well as no one knew what charms and secret lore, had to spend so much of

24

their early life in study that they were never young, but usually forceful; but Illtud complained of the cold and laid out his stiff leg with painful care. He read Mennor's written packet with a shaking head and said that things were nothing like as bad as that.

'Eh? What things?' asked Rhodri.

Illtud gave him a quick glance and said, 'Well, you know Mennor, always an alarmist. You want to take his tales with a pinch of salt, Brannock.'

One did not contradict an elder. Brannock said carefully, 'I am not asked for an opinion, Illtud.'

'Well, I've given you mine. And as for helping you on your way, that's impossible. You can see this lame leg of mine wouldn't cover one mile, let alone seven.'

'Mennor's instructions—' Brannock began.

'Then you'd better go back to Mennor,' Illtud interrupted. 'Or manage alone.'

He looked at Rhodri, who said nodding, 'Or stay here a few days and make us a proper visit. Always pleased to see you, you know!'

He filled their cups all round, and Brannock sat confounded. Iorwenna came in then, asking hospitably if they had all they wanted, and caught Brannock's eye and nodded to the door. When she had gone he rose and said good-night, and Rhodri, assuming that he had accepted Illtud's refusal, said affectionately, 'That's a sensible lad!'

Iorwenna was waiting for him outside. 'I'm sorry,' she said, 'I forgot that you don't know Illtud well. My dear, there's nothing he won't do to avoid stirring himself. You should have asked me.'

'He was *pleased* to refuse me,' said Brannock, smarting.

'No, it was to annoy Mennor. They never did

25

agree. But don't you worry about being put on your way. I'll send one of the children.'

Brannock was a hero to her gaggle of boys, who were all younger, and he went to bed cheered. Iorwenna woke him next morning before dawn, saying into his ear, 'Get up quietly.'

When he had pulled his clothes on and followed her, still half-asleep and puzzled, she said comfortably, 'You'll avoid argument if you go before anyone is awake. Eat your breakfast while we fetch your horse, and give me your food-bag and I'll see you have plenty for the journey.'

Waiting for him outside in the misty dawn-light, already mounted and holding his horse, was a small muffled figure he took to be the eldest of the boys; but Iorwenna, coming out with two food-bags, said, 'Here you are, and this is Eilian's.'

'Eilian?' said Brannock, disagreeably surprised. Eilian was the eldest child and the only daughter, whom he knew only vaguely as a skinny girl with a stream of red hair, generally engaged in scolding the boys.

'She's the only one I can trust to be sensible. Look after Brannock, Eilian, I'll manage without you somehow.'

Brannock suppressed his offence at being consigned to the care of a girl, and they walked their horses quietly into the mist. It was brightening fast, and would be a fair day soon. As they came clear of the village street they quickened to a trot, and Brannock shook off his bad temper. He had successfully surmounted the first obstacle in his way, and as soon as this girl had brought him to the right spot and taken herself home he could resort to his bob, and with his bob he always felt confident. Here was Brannock

26

king's son riding on an important errand, handsome horse, handsome dog – he gave a touch to his cloak and shook back his hair on his shoulders; and then that fool Goldeneye rocketed past them barking madly.

There was a ford ahead of them, marked by an old hollow willow, and among its autumn shower of yellow leaves Goldeneye was leaping wildly about. Brannock called him to heel, quite uselessly. Eilian trotted past him, reined in under the tree, and said into its branches, 'Well, aren't you clever!'

What looked like a knob of willow-branch rose, arched its back, and yawned pinkly. This drove Goldeneye into a frenzy. Brannock broke off a willow-wand and hit him, saying savagely, 'It's nothing but a cat, you fool!' and kicked his horse angrily through the ford.

Behind him he heard Eilian saying goodbye to the cat more lovingly than she had to her mother. When she came up beside him again he said sourly, 'That animal won't follow us, I hope. I haven't trained my dog to be patient with cats.' Which was true.

Eilian said politely, 'Please don't worry about Pangur. He can deal with dogs. And he was only seeing me off. Cats can't travel more than three or four miles a day.' He noticed that she had not troubled to dress as befitted a king's daughter accompanying a king's son; her cloak was rough with thorn-pulls and her tunic a most unbecoming colour. She took, poor child, after her father rather than her mother, and was sparrow-boned, with a blank little face like a bird's egg with a sharp nose stuck to it, and marigold-coloured hair too straight and shiny to stay in a plait.

'And it's seven miles you have to guide me?'

'Seven miles to the place where the elders meet.'

A suspicious thought occurred to him. 'But I thought this place was meant to be secret.'

'Oh, meant!' she said with slight scorn. 'Illtud takes such care of himself, making out he's too lame to carry his own bag or walk the distance. So someone has to go with him to bring back the horses, and then meet him again on the way back.'

'Oh? So you've seen the elders starting on this journey of theirs?'

'I think he pretends he's walked. He always tells me to go away quickly.' Disappointed, he was silent. She looked at him consideringly and repeated, 'He always *tells* me.'

'What? You don't?'

'Well, would you?'

For the first time he allowed himself to smile. 'Then can you show me?'

She said primly, 'I don't know why you want to know.'

'Mennor sent me to follow their path.'

'Then why didn't he give you a charm to show you how?'

A disagreeably direct girl! He said stiffly, 'It's not for me to explain.'

She pursed her lips in a way that reminded him of his mother, but said only, 'I can show you as much as I have seen.'

They rode on in silence. It was pleasant wooded country, rising from the borders of Eastmark towards the long brown hills of the waste. Eilian seemed to be sighting on some point of these hills; presently the trees on their left began to thin out, and soon they were picking their way over long shallow ribs of grey rock running down from the north. It was nearing noon when Eilian halted and slid to the ground, giving him her rein and saying, 'Wait here, I have to find it on foot.'

She went off in an irritatingly vague manner, first one way and then another. Brannock had expected a standing stone or a hoar tree, but the place seemed no different from what they had ridden through for the last mile. To make his temper even shorter, Goldeneye went with her, leaping at her with puppyish barks. Finally she took her stand at what seemed no particular spot and turned to him nodding.

They stood on a brown moor. To the north the ribs of rock ran up into a huddle of gentle hills, mostly treeless, with some bright specks of flowering gorse. He said coldly, 'This can be no meeting-place.'

She turned up the blank little egg-face and looked at him hard; but only said quietly, 'If you'll dismount I can show you.'

He got down ungraciously, and with care she moved him to the spot where she had stood. 'You line up the rock-edge on your left with the crest of the skyline; then the boulder over there with the nick on the top of the hill. Now—' she looked up at the sun – 'now look due north.'

He stared at the hills. They were not such a formless huddle as he had thought. Perhaps a shred or two of mist had blown away from them? Directly ahead of him lay a gap that was a plain way in. He took a step to his left and it was gone; a step back, and there it was.

'Well,' he said, forgetting to be haughty, 'that could be charmed or it could be a trick of the light. You've been that way?'

Eilian shook her head vigorously. 'I was supposed to go home before the elders had all arrived. But I was riding a good horse that day, and I took him for a gallop, over there, on the left of the hills, and when I stopped to breathe my horse I was high enough to see where the elders were going.'

Brannock studied the ground. From this exact spot of the meeting-place, the little huddle of hills now looked less formless; it was a compact formation, from this angle roughly circular, perhaps fifteen miles across at its broadest, standing like a low fortification in the rolling plain. And from the west side, where Eilian had exercised her horse, a gentle rise would have given her a limited view into the fortification.

'Yes, I see. So which way were they going?'

'A fair bit north of west. But wait! They were a way west of the meeting-place then. And they were disappearing into a wood. And when I'd let my horse graze and had something to eat myself, the elders had gone and so had the wood.'

She sat on her heels and drew in the dust. 'Here's this meeting-place; here's the way in, due north of it; and here's where they were, west of the way in and heading north of west. And here's the wood that disappeared. What I thought was, they went in, and then made a very wide bend, first left and then right; as if they were to go in a circle.'

Brannock looked down at her drawing and up at the hills in front of them. 'Yes, the hills look as if they make a circle. Then the quickest way for us would be to ride to the top of the left-hand hill. Come on. We can stop at the top to eat.'

He held out his hand to pull her up, but she hung back. She looked a little shocked. 'Shouldn't you go the proper way?'

'Why? This will be quicker. We can see the path from the top of the hill, and save time by going straight down to it.'

'Well—' she said dubiously, but got up and let him mount her. Once up, she objected, 'The wood disappeared. There must have been some charm at work.'

'The whole thing is a charm, if you ask me. Ready?'

She kicked her horse on, but so unwillingly that he let her go first and swung in behind to urge her on. They rode north for half a mile or so, sheered off to the left to skirt the hill, and then turned up it.

It was curiously hard going. Although from the meeting-place the slope had looked slight and even, soon their canter had fallen to a laboured trot. Moreover, though he could not understand how he had failed to see it from below, they were among the ribs of rock again, higher than ever before, so that their way now twisted below miniature precipices, with no view in any direction. The day seemed to darken; he looked up, and suddenly he was sweating, and there was a singing in his head. He dropped his eyes at once, concentrating fiercely between his horse's ears, able to think of nothing but keeping his seat. Eilian, riding ahead of him, looked oddly squat under her cloak. She was leaning on her horse's neck, of course, on a slope that was too steep to ride, and even Goldeneye was running oddly, low to the ground with tail and ears down. He called, 'We must walk!' and slid off. Because of the singing in his head he landed clumsily, with a jar that made him gasp, so that Goldeneye turned to look at him. Goldeneye grinned at him, and advanced on him, and he was not Goldeneye but a red-eyed wolf. At the same moment Eilian's back rose into vast hooked wings that turned with a hiss and bore down on him.

His horse reared, screaming, and knocked him

spinning. He lay where he fell, hiding his eyes; he knew why he should have taken the proper way.

Presently Goldeneye came and pushed him worriedly with his wet nose. He uncovered enough of an eye to be sure that he was Goldeneye again, and sat up and looked around.

Eilian was holding both horses and quietly stroking them. She gave him his reins and said, 'You can do as you like but I am leaving this hill.' The little egg-face was greenish-white, but she was quite calm.

They led their horses down to the gentler slope, mounted, and rode round the skirts of the hill and half a mile south to the meeting-place of the elders. They had wasted two hours.

Three

They left the horses to graze and made their midday meal in silence. Brannock said at last, 'The elders don't ride, do they?'

'No.'

'Then will you take my horse back with you?'

'Yes,' said Eilian in relief. She added, 'You'll have to carry two day's food. That's what Illtud always took.'

'I've enough for that.'

He found the spot from which the entrance could be seen and took out his bob. Watching, Eilian asked, 'What are you doing?'

'Using the charm as Mennor told me to.'

He rubbed his fingers and let the bob swing free. It was dead at first; then he thought of stepping back so that it hung over the right spot. At once he felt the tingle begin in his fingers, and the bob swung heavily, directly towards the entrance.

'So that's your pathfinder!' said Eilian. She came cautiously up to him and put her fingers lightly on his hand, and then took them away startled. 'It stings!'

'Can you do it?'

He guided her hand to the right place, but as soon as he let it go the bob fell still. She shook her head. 'No, it isn't given to me to work it. What's this weight?' She polished it on her sleeve and blinked at it in surprise. 'Why, it's my brooch!'

'A brooch, yes, an old one Mennor found.'

'But exactly like mine, look.' She pulled forward the brooch that held the cloak on her shoulder. He had noticed it before, thinking it sadly old-fashioned, though heavy and well-worked. It was well-worn too, but there was the same pattern of fine lines running round it, with the red colouring almost complete on the intricate lacings in the splayed ends.

Polishing these too, she said, 'No one knows how old it is, but it always goes to the eldest daughter of the family. I was glad I got it rather than your Ingaret . . . . Don't you trust your elder either?'

'What?' he said, startled.

'Well, no one could trust Illtud. He's for ever leading my father into troubles my mother has to put right.'

'What kind of troubles?' Brannock asked thoughtfully.

'Political. He tried to stir up mischief in the other kingdoms, in the hope of taking them over. There was a nasty friend of his with us for weeks not long ago, until Mother said that if he didn't go she would.'

'Was his name Petrock?'

'A friend of Mennor's too?'

'No. Mennor's all right, and he didn't like Petrock. I don't think he knew Petrock had been here. . . . I wish he had. What makes you think I don't trust him?'

'You don't want to use the charm he gave you.'

'Oh,' said Brannock, at this truth he had not quite seen for himself. He coiled the thong and put away the bob. 'It isn't Mennor I don't trust,' he said at last, 'and it isn't *his* charm. He didn't give it to me; he told me to use it.'

'You said he did give it to you.'

'Only the brooch; the charm works as well with

anything. I've always been able to do it, but I don't know why. I don't know why, and I don't know how, and I'm—'

This was not easy to say. He thought of the hooked wings rising from Eilian's back and Goldeneye's evil grin. He said, 'I am afraid to trust it. Eilian, will you come with me?'

She went greenish-pale again; but well before he had got the question out, so that he saw that she had known he would ask it. All she said was, 'Will your charm answer questions?'

'I don't think so. What question?'

'Whether it will let me go with you. Well,' she said, blinking with apprehension, 'if it won't I expect it will send me back. Let's see to the food-bags.'

In the everyday business of food and grazing he shook off his fears. Before they had eaten and repacked, he was wondering why he had saddled himself with the irritating little creature.

There was a difficulty about the horses. Eilian said that hers would find its own way home; Brannock doubted his, which in any case had farther to go. 'Oh, I'll speak to him,' Eilian said casually. She went between the two of them, pulled their heads to her, and spent some time stroking and murmuring. When she let them go with a couple of smart slaps, they trotted off together without hesitation.

'Can you do charms, then?' Brannock asked.

'Only the usual ones; like asking the seeds to grow and the bees to stay well-disposed to us and so on.'

'Wouldn't those things happen without charms?'

'Sometimes. They don't always happen even with the charms. But it's rude not to say them.'

'Rude?'

'You want them to oblige you, don't you? We make direct for the entrance now, do we?'

They shouldered their bags and set off. Brannock was in two minds about her effect on the horses. She said her own would go home of its own accord, and wasn't it natural that his would follow, at least for a time? She was a helpful little thing, and he had to admit that her calmness was praiseworthy (though he did not believe that she had seen the hooked wings and the wolf's grin); but she was annoyingly self-opinionated. Besides, this was *his* errand; why should he share the glory at the end of it?

And if there was no glory and he made a fool of himself, he wanted no girl watching.

He had thought that there was a blossoming broom-bush in front of the entrance, but as they came nearer it turned out to be a standing stone reared in the way. Eilian muttered, 'That wasn't there before,' and showed reluctance to go near it, so that it was easy for him to be bold.

'Pass it sunwise,' he advised her, and went directly to it – though carefully on its left side – and laid both hands on it. At once he forgot about impressing Eilian, for the stone tingled to him in friendliness. It was about his own height, very roughly shaped, and as firm as the land itself. At eye-height on the southern face something had once been carved, but that had long ago been worn away, leaving only a shallow circular dip with what might have been a cross inside it. 'We're on the right path,' he said; 'it's friendly; come and touch it.'

'To me too?' she said warily, and used only a finger-tip. 'Oh, that's how it feels when you're holding your bob. This must be the right path, then. And since

36

nothing has come at me—' she looked apprehensively above her head – 'I suppose I can go in.'

They passed the stone on their right hand. They were in a shallow valley with turfy downs on either side; it did not lead due north, but inclined gently to their left. It was a pleasant way in the afternoon sun. Goldeneye rambled happily around them, and Eilian began to hum scraps of tunes under her breath. When they had been walking for some time without trouble, Brannock said, 'What was it that came at you, up on the hill?' There seemed no reason for it, but he kept his voice low.

'Something it isn't wise to talk about.'

'Yes, but what I saw—' She flashed a dangerous look at him, and he said, 'Yes, all right, but – it wasn't strange to me.'

'Of course it wasn't,' she said sharply. 'You were meant to be frightened.' She refused to say any more. It was quite a long time before he realized that the red-eyed wolf would have been much less terrible if it had not been Goldeneye.

Presently he pointed out, 'We've turned right-handed.'

Eilian looked up at the sun, frowning. 'We have, but I didn't notice it. We're going north again. And look ahead – we'll be turning north-east soon.'

'You saw the elders turn north into a wood. We've seen no wood.'

'The wood must have been a charm to hide them. I think we're going in a circle.'

He got out his bob as a precaution, and it directed them on, always turning slowly right-handed. And after all, he found, it was good to have someone to talk to. They exchanged family news, and discovered that they agreed very well; both had brothers who

37

exasperated them, and could sing the same songs, and Eilian played chasing games with Goldeneye without the least hint that he was disobedient. This pleased Brannock so much that he even allowed her to tell him some stories about the intelligence of her cat, though they seemed to him to have little point.

Quite suddenly, the season reminded him that it was no longer summer. They were in the shadow of the hills on their right, and the evening air struck cold.

'We're going *south*!' he said, startled.

'Yes. The way is a circle, then. A big one; we must have come twenty miles. And we'd better get on, because this is no place to spend the night.'

It was not. There was no shelter, no wood for a fire, and, worst of all, no water. 'We've enough for tonight,' said Brannock, 'but we can't expect streams in this downland country.'

'The country will change.'

'How do you know?'

'Illtud never took more than one water-bottle.'

They increased their pace. Their way now swung a little towards the west, but the hills on their right turned sharply across their way, in a barrier that, black against the cold western sky, seemed suddenly too high and threatening for downland. Sharp tongues of rock began to appear through the turf, and in the increasing dusk the going became difficult.

'Time for the bob,' said Brannock. They had to peer to see which way it swung. Unbelievably, it directed them now left-handedly. They tried again a quarter of a mile on, and the answer was the same.

'Another bend?' Eilian said. 'And the other way?'

'But much smaller. We'd better hold hands, it's getting very rough.'

38

It was all rock now, and on their left they seemed to be skirting a high black shoulder. 'We must find shelter,' Brannock said after some stumbles, 'this is too dangerous in the dark. We'll follow one of these clefts until it narrows. Keep to the light side, or you'll slip.'

Eilian said unhappily, 'We wasted too much time this morning.'

It was Brannock who slipped, coming down atrociously hard on his stomach into a narrow gap. Gasping ignominiously, he was conscious of Eilian landing neatly at his side.

'Only winded?' she said cheerfully.

Only winded! He might have broken a leg. He had severely bruised his shin, probably he *had* broken a leg, and all she could do—

Luckily he had no breath to say all this, for his wheezings with his face to the ground brought him a familiar smell. He flapped a hand speechlessly, scraped something up, and held it towards her.

'Charcoal!' she said on a gasp, and vanished. When he could sit up he propped himself against a rock and heard her moving in the darkness, and Goldeneye's claws scraping nearby. Then a faint red glow, followed by licking flames, lit up a flat stone with the scars of burning on it, and her small figure kneeling and feeding the fire. When he could summon a strangled thread of voice, he asked, 'Where did you find wood?'

'A pile at the back there, plenty. And I can hear water, we'll find it in the morning. Get your breath while I make supper.'

They ate comfortably by the light of a good red fire, Goldeneye curled between them. The sides of the gap were deep enough to shelter them from weather, and

39

it had been neatly cleared, the hearth-stone set in the centre, and kindling and logs stacked at one end. 'It's the elders' regular resting place,' Eilian said certainly.

'We would have reached it in the light if we had started earlier. It will be easier tomorrow, we must travel faster than they do.'

She said after a time, in an irritatingly sententious way, 'I think we are being led.'

The fire was beginning to sink. Brannock reached over for his blanket, and threw Eilian hers. 'That's nonsense. You don't think even Mennor could set a charm to make me fall off a rock he didn't know I would be on?'

Eilian brushed the embers into the centre of the fire, tidied the food-bags, and rolled herself into her blanket. 'No, I don't,' she said, wriggling into a comfortable spot. 'Any more than I think it's the elders who are directing your bob. It's the land itself that's doing it.'

'The land?' said Brannock; but Eilian was asleep. He pulled the blanket up to his chin and called Goldeneye to his side to share their warmth. The land? He supposed that it was the land that controlled his bob, and surely it was the land that made the entrance-stone feel friendly.

He remembered some things that Mennor had said. *The hall of my Order is protected by a secret of the land itself. Do you really imagine that any charm I could make would be stronger than that?*

And again: *You have the favour of the land.*

It should have been comforting. In a way it was comforting. And in a way he had always known it, never in his life having had a moment's fear that the land could harm him. But he had not understood how much that meant. It is not entirely comforting to have the favour of something that turns out to be demanding beyond comprehension. It is not in the least comforting to abandon yourself wholly to the care of a weight on a piece of string.

But he supposed, as he settled down to sleep, that he would get used to it. It was only in his last waking moment that he remembered his mother's words. *The land may have its own wants.*

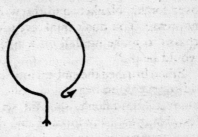

Four

It was strange to wake in the morning to a place they had not seen before, high black rocks, green with dripping water. The weather too had changed, with low sullen clouds and little wind. There was no time to coax a bright fire, so they breakfasted cold and found a trickle of water to fill their bottles.

'The bob,' said Brannock when they had climbed down from their shelter to the rocky floor of the valley. The ground was so broken that there was no obvious way.

The bob directed them north-east. Eilian at first refused to believe it, arguing that it must mean south-west.

'We've *come* that way.'

'But on the other side of the rocks up there.'

'But if it swings back and forth, how do you know which way it means?'

This had never occurred to Brannock. He let the bob swing free again, watching it. No, there was nothing to be seen, but he could feel it; the weight of the swing was to the north-east.

'Well,' Eilian said philosophically, 'if this is meant to hide the way to the hall of the Order we can't expect it to be straightforward. North-east it is.'

North-east it was for a time; and then north, and north-west, and west. 'Circling again,' Brannock said tiredly, 'and this time the other way; counter-sunwise. I thought that was wrong.'

'It is,' Eilian said, irritatingly know-all. 'You should never go round sacred things counter-sunwise.'

'Well, the bob says we have to.'

'That's the only reason I'm doing it.'

Their happy travelling of the day before was gone. They were both wet, cold and ill-tempered. The cloud had thickened and lowered until they were in a blind dripping mist, and over such broken ground they had to stop continually to use the bob. Often they could follow it for no more than fifty yards before they had to leave the way to scramble round a boulder the size of a hut, or splash through an icy stream that flowed first one way and then the other. Eilian, being small, came off worse, and it slightly cheered Brannock that he had to help her more than once over a long step or a steep climb. Even Goldeneye was subdued, and padded at heel instead of leaping around them. When they could go no farther, they huddled under a rock to eat the remains of breakfast, pulling Goldeneye between them for some warmth.

Thinking longingly of last night's fire and hot supper, Brannock said, 'You can do charms. Couldn't you charm away some of this mist?' He was not, to tell the truth, very hopeful. There seemed a great deal of the mist and very little of Eilian, and though it was generally accepted that the women could set weather-charms they very seldom agreed to do so.

Eilian said in a depressed way, 'I'd been wondering if I could. I don't know if a charm I made alone would be strong enough. And I don't think I have everything I need.'

He did not ask what she needed, because that was

women's business, and the women were secretive about such things, but offered, 'Is there something I can find here?'

'No, it's chiefly herbs.' She turned her back on him while she ferreted in her bag, and presently stood up with her hands cupped.

'I hope it won't hurt to try. I'll have to use vervain instead of rue, and some things I haven't got at all. You wait here.'

She shook herself and stepped away from him into the mist. He pulled warm Goldeneye closer, rumpling his ears, and Goldeneye put a heavy paw on his arm and panted in pleasure.

Dreamily, he thought that they had been sitting like this for a surprisingly long time.

Goldeneye sprang to his feet. The hair on his shoulders was bristling, and he was staring in the direction in which Eilian had vanished – how long ago?

Brannock scrambled to his feet and called, 'Eilian!' No charm could surely take so long to set? But would he break it if he went after her?

A hill of mist rolled down on him, so thick that he could not see Goldeneye two paces in front of him. He flailed stupidly at it, took a step forward, and fetched up against a boulder he was sure had not been there before. He shouted again, and Goldeneye, a cheerful Goldeneye with his hackles down, bounded on him. He cuffed him down and demanded, 'Where is Eilian?' Goldeneye rushed in a circle and went down on his elbows with a silly inviting bark. *Find!* Brannock shouted at him. Goldeneye sat up and panted, looking past him. He turned and saw Eilian sitting cross-legged on the ground.

'What happened?' he asked.

She said, 'Well, I didn't charm the mist away.' She looked a little dazed.

'The mist got worse.'

'Yes, it did, didn't it. Perhaps it didn't like that I used vervain instead of rue.'

'Why should one herb rather than another make any difference?'

She got to her feet and shook herself, tenderly, as if the failed charm had bruised her. 'It might be that rue only grows in places where the weather is changeable. Or it might be that it isn't the herb that matters so much as the effort I should have made to find it.'

'No one could have found rue here.'

'Then perhaps I shouldn't have tried to charm without it. Anyway, I failed. Where's your bob?'

They started again the wearying business of taking their direction every few hundred yards. Each asking took them left-handedly, and Brannock said, 'If we ever see the sun again we shall surely find that we are going south-west, if not south. There, that way now, a little clear ground for once.'

He stopped to put away the bob, and Eilian said, 'Oh good!' and stepped out in front of him.

Before her the wall of mist split like a sliced apple, and a crimson gleam of sunset shone from jagged black rocks forty feet below.

Eilian stopped on her toes on the brink, arms out as she toppled. Brannock jumped to catch her from behind. Breathless together, they looked down into a cleft where the tops of trees growing on its side waved beneath their feet.

At last Brannock said, 'We had best stay here until morning.'

The mist closed down again. Eilian said in an undertone, 'Thank you!' Feeling their way foot by foot, they found a corner between rocks and huddled there, sharing some dry bread-cakes; they heard Goldeneye's share going down in two snaps.

Brannock whispered in the darkness, 'Did your charm force away the mist after all?'

He heard a stir as she shook her head, but there was a silence before she said, 'You don't understand about charms.'

'Then *tell* me.'

'They don't force things. You *ask*.'

'But you said you weren't strong enough to charm away the mist.'

'One request isn't much. No – you don't exactly ask; it's too difficult to explain. You have to – to remember that you are part of it, and – and lean your weight in the way you want it to go. That's why it's important to set the charm properly. It makes you feel – reminds you that you are part of it.'

'But part of *what*?'

He heard her sigh, but whether at him or at herself he was not certain. 'I don't know. Of everything you are trying to charm. Of whatever it is that you must say thank you to when your charm has worked.'

He was grateful for the darkness then, for he knew he was going red in a terrible blush of shame. When she had spoken her thanks on the edge of the ravine, he had thought they were for him. Had he said anything to give away his mistake?

'But I don't understand why you ask,' she went on sleepily. 'Whatever it is, you must know it better than

I do. It's what allows your bob to work, isn't it? Isn't it the land itself?'

He was too busy resenting his shame to answer her.

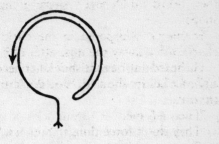

Five

In the morning the mist was gone and everything looked different. In particular, the ravine looked almost harmless.

'If you'd gone over,' Brannock said self-righteously, 'you'd have got no more than a few bruises. Look, Goldeneye's over in a couple of jumps.'

Goldeneye was capering on the opposite bank, urging them on. Eilian gave him a hard look, but only stood back for him to go first. When he had crossed the noisy little stream at the bottom, he saw her standing upright at the edge and speaking, but not to him. When she caught up with him, he asked uneasily, 'What were you saying up there?'

She said without looking at him, 'Plainly you see no need for thanks.'

No need! What about thanks to him, who had stopped her pitching over? Even if it was only a couple of bruises that he had saved her. They went on in cold silence. In spite of the sun the wind had a chill in it. They left the rocks behind, and on their right the slopes were covered with a beech forest, shining red and bronze in the clear day. After a time he pointed out, 'I was right, wasn't I? We're going west now, and you can see that this valley is turning south soon.'

'Yes,' she said.

'Well,' he returned, since she would not be friendly,

'what about food? You should have noticed that we have very little left.'

She said stubbornly, 'We brought as much as Illtud always carried. It's not my fault that we've been slower than the elders.'

'I suppose it was mine!'

'There will be nuts in the beech-wood, and I still have meal left; I can make bread-cakes when we light a fire. Can't your dog hunt?'

'I wouldn't have a dog that couldn't,' he said, offended again, and sheered off up the right-hand slope. She called after him instantly in alarm, and he enjoyed taking no notice. Getting high enough to scan the land ahead, he trotted down and said briskly, 'This valley grows broader and the stream grows marshy a mile or so farther on, and there are gorse coverts. We'll find coney or duck there. You go uphill and collect nuts, and we'll meet by the marshes.'

The little egg-face had turned pinched with anxiety. 'You know we shouldn't leave the way along the valley.'

'It didn't hurt me,' he said brazenly, 'so you'll be all right. Off you go, and don't be too long about it.'

She went so silently that he called after her, 'I did take care not to go high.'

She trailed off dispiritedly, so that he had to assure himself that he had not been unkind.

It was a good place among the marshes, and to his inexpressible fury Goldeneye revelled in it, dashing in an aureole of beaten-up water through and through the reedy pools until any game would have disappeared. There were no water-birds to be seen, and conies, he recalled too late, would not have been feeding at this time of day. He called Goldeneye back in a rage, but by the time he arrived, in a series of wild

49

circles, had grown more sensible. Of course Golden-eye was a hunting dog, but he had been trained – well, partly trained – in the village drives; and in any case there was no game here.

But there were clumps of mushrooms. He collected them into his bag, and then found an island of blackberry bushes, and stripped them into a pouch of dock-leaves. By the time Eilian arrived, with the bag heavy on her shoulder, he had grown so cheerful that he forgot they were quarrelling, and gave her a generous half of the berries to eat as they walked. Also, because she did not ask about the hunting, he told her the truth about it.

'Goldeneye can't live on mushrooms,' she objected. Seeing her eating, Goldeneye was trotting at her side, uttering small coaxing barks. She gave him a black-berry, which disappointed him.

'Then that will teach him to hunt, I hope. The conies will come out to feed at dusk, and he'll be hungrier by then. Time for the bob, I think.'

It confirmed their way, and Eilian, nodding up at the beech-slopes, said, 'From up there you can see that we shall have to turn in about three miles. This hill on our left seems to bend easterly.'

Brannock pondered as they walked. The stream had deepened, and was sliding silently between under-cut banks thick with old willows, whose falling yellow leaves showered and eddied around them. Hopeful that they might be eatable, Goldeneye pursued them energetically.

'How far do you think we've come?'

Eilian looked doubtful. 'From the stone in the entrance? Difficult to say in that bad going yesterday. Thirty-five miles at least.'

'Yes. And at first bending always to our right, and

50

then round the rocky place where the elders slept, and after that always bending to the left, do you think?'

'I'm not sure of that in the mist. But since this morning we've made almost half a circle left-handedly.'

'Then,' said Brannock in secret triumph, 'shall I tell you what will happen in the next turn? We shall go right-handed round the shoulder of this hill on the right, and once we are round that we shall be going north-west, always inclining to our right, until we go due north.'

She turned on him a satisfyingly puzzled look.

'No, I shan't tell you how I know. Wait until we get there.'

A little later he changed this to, 'Wait until we see if I'm right.'

But they did not see it, for the stream turned away from them sharply. Eilian stopped to fill the water-bottles, saying practically, 'We don't know when we shall find water again. And look, the beech-woods have come right across the valley. We shall have a comfortable camp tonight.'

But they had a slow walk, because under the canopy of bronze leaves they had no other guide than that of the bob. Getting along patiently in this way, Brannock realized how completely he had lost his sense of direction. Normally he could stray at random all day through the land, and still have in the back of his mind the point where home lay. Now he did not know where his home was, and he could not have said where they had been half an hour back. It surprised him to find that this did not worry him; he was quite content to trust to the guidance of the bob.

There were beech-leaves everywhere, fluttering down upon them, lying in great leather-brown drifts in every dip. Brannock went waist-deep into one heap, let out a yell of alarm, and then froze in shame. He was trying to gather some dignity when Goldeneye hurtled to his rescue and they both went head over heels, wrestling and sneezing. Something launched itself into the air above them, and Eilian crashed shrieking into the deepest of the drift and started scooping leaves to bury them. When they remembered that they were messengers on an important errand they scrambled out, shook themselves free of leaves, and went on giggling. What did dignity matter, after all? Brannock began to sing, and Eilian joined him. The bob directed them through the big shadowy tree trunks until the dusk was thick around them, and Eilian, predictably, began to worry about Goldeneye's supper.

'Conies, boy! Go find 'em!'

Charmed by the attention, Goldeneye leapt at her and began a wrestling game. Brannock clouted him off, picked Eilian up, and told her not to worry.

'But he must be so hungry!'

'Let him hunt, then,' said Brannock heartlessly. 'And I'm hungry too and it's almost dark. Let's make camp.'

They found a good spot under the roots of an enormous beech, and while Eilian kindled the fire Brannock went to collect wood. Goldeneye followed, but he chased him off in disgust. How hungry did the silly beast have to be before it occurred to him to do something about it? Snapping dead wood under his heel was a noisy business, but through it he thought he heard something else, a kind of ghost of Goldeneye's bustling. He put down the firewood and went to look for him.

Goldeneye was standing with his hackles raised,

looking – there was no better word for it – confused; but at his foot lay a newly killed pigeon.

'Supper!' shouted Brannock, hugged him tumultuously, and pelted back to Eilian.

One pigeon is not much between three, but together with breads and nuts and mushrooms it made them very happy; Brannock not least because at last his dog had justified his boasts about him. 'A coney,' he said judicially, 'would have been better, but a pigeon was acceptable. A coney tomorrow, Goldeneye, if you please.' Sprawled on his side, Goldeneye thumped his tail lazily.

Staring at the trees over their heads, Eilian shaded her eyes from the light of the fire and sat sharply up. 'Look! Stars!'

They stared and calculated, and Brannock puffed himself a little. 'So we turned the corner of the hill while we were in these woods. We've been going west.'

It completed a happy evening for him to see Eilian impressed. 'But how did you know?'

He was happy enough to admit, 'I didn't know; it just seemed a good guess.' He turned on his elbow, swept a space on the ground clear, and started to draw with a twig. 'This is the way we've come. North from the entrance stone, and then in two circles, first sunwise and then turning outwards to counter-sunwise. Now I guess that we are turning outwards again into a third circle sunwise. There, like that. Does that remind you of anything?'

She looked at it blankly.

'Haven't you a troy in your village?'

'Oh. . . . There was one, but it's all overgrown. There were stones that marked the beginning, but one of the men took them away for building. Illtud said he

53

would have bad luck if he did, but he didn't take any notice.'

'Did he have bad luck?'

'His girl wouldn't marry him because she wouldn't live in a hut built on troy-stones. The grandmothers said we should put the troy to rights, but they couldn't agree about the way it went, and the men laughed at them and it came to nothing. They say there used to be an eve-of-spring dance there, but no one remembers how it should go.'

'Our girls say it was a dancing-game, and they still try to dance it sometimes, but they forget more of it every year. One half of ours is covered by brambles, but you can still see the turf-lines on the other half, and I think they make a pattern like this.' He pored over his drawing on the ground. '*Something* like this. There's a difference, but I can't remember—'

Eilian said practically, 'Do you know what it was like in the middle?'

'What? No, that was all gone.'

'Then it won't help us. What does it matter? We've got the bob. Go to sleep.'

Six

Brannock was surprised to find himself awake before dawn. Hoisting himself on his elbow, he found that he had rolled out of his blanket and was cramped with cold. Uttering complaining noises under his breath, he pulled himself over to stir some warmth out of the embers of the fire, and saw that Goldeneye was missing.

In the night the wind had risen. It was hissing through the tree-tops far above, though down here in their shelter only a few stray leaves lifted and whirled. One of the whirls as he looked at it became Goldeneye, upright and taut, watching something out in the darkness.

Eilian was sleeping peacefully. He got cautiously to his feet and went to investigate. Goldeneye greeted him politely, yawned, and went back to the fire and curled himself up to sleep. Puzzled, Brannock climbed out of the shelter and listened.

There was nothing to hear but the fretting of the wind, but he judged that it was near dawn; light enough, anyway, to collect more firewood, so that it would be warm for Eilian when she woke, and she could get breakfast all the sooner.

He found a good armful of wood, took it back to the camp, and knelt to build up the embers. Needing kindling, he felt for the pile Eilian had left last night. His hand found something limp and furry and cold. It was a dead coney.

He peered at Eilian in the growing light. She slept curled into a ball, and under her chin was curled another ball, a striped one.

He said aloud in disgust, 'Oh no!'

Eilian woke, sneezed into the striped fur, and said in pleasure, 'Pangur, you clever cat!'

The cat Pangur yawned without opening his eyes, recoiled himself with a paw over his nose, and went to sleep again.

Brannock looked despairingly at Goldeneye, heaved a sigh, and said, 'I think Pangur caught the pigeon last night.'

Eilian embraced Goldeneye and said, 'Pigeons are difficult for dogs and easy for cats. See to the fire while I skin the coney.'

It was dawning a sharp clear morning, and he made a good roaring fire. Eilian was annoyingly thrifty with the coney. 'We ate well last night and we shall be hungry this evening.' She allowed them each a joint, roasted on hot stones, and sent him off to find leaves to wrap the rest of it. While they ate, Pangur slept undisturbed.

'That's all right,' Eilian said. 'He will have hunted for himself first.'

'A dog wouldn't,' Brannock said defensively.

'Yes, cats are different. But don't you see that this proves you right? We are following a troy-game.'

'Why?'

'Because Pangur found us. He couldn't have followed us; a cat couldn't cover forty miles in three days. But if this is a troy and we are on the western edge of it, we could be as little as seven miles from home.'

Brannock did not much consider cats, which to him belonged solely in the barn and the kitchen, but the

56

pigeon and the coney made him generous. He offered, 'I could help you carry him.'

'He wouldn't like that,' Eilian said firmly. 'It was good of him to come and hunt for us, but now we'll leave him here. He'll find his way home when he wants to. Now we mustn't waste the day. See that the fire is properly out.'

She was, he thought, kicking a hole for the embers and stamping them in, getting into a disagreeably womanly habit of ordering him about. He was glad that, having the bob, he was in final control of this journey. She said a sentimental goodbye to Pangur, who took no notice at all, and Brannock, remembering his manners, ran two fingers down his striped back and said, 'Thank you, Pangur.' They climbed out of their shelter and he took out the bob to find their direction. Watching it swing, and looking up at the cold sky to check that the way was northerly he said, 'Yes, I do think that we are travelling a troy-game. But Eilian – do you feel that we are only seven miles from your home?'

'No, I don't. And not because we've walked so far, either. I feel that we are outside.'

'Outside what?'

'I don't know. We are inside the troy, so it doesn't matter where else we aren't. Come on, it looks easy walking this morning.'

The sun was driving away the chill of the night, and after an hour they came out of the beech-woods to more open country full of small streams, great banks of briar in full fruit, and slopes open to the sun where the nuts were ripening. Goldeneye, ecstatic in the water, pounced on them down muddy banks, and it was difficult not to chase him. They found themselves marooned on what they were certain was not an

57

island, and got very wet getting off it, and had to stop
for half an hour at noon to spread their cloaks in the
sun to dry. There were cresses in the streams, and
Eilian (of course) had collected nuts, so they could eat
without fear for the evening. When they started again,
Brannock found wild thyme, and brought it to her to
flavour their supper.

'There should be garlic along these streams,' she
said. 'Go that way, Brannock, and I'll go this, and see
if you can find some. But not too far, I don't think we
should separate.'

She went off skipping and humming, and Goldeneye, after some tearing between them, fell in with his
tongue out at Brannock's heel. Brannock jumped the
stream and skirted its bank, humming too and not
very much in earnest about the garlic, which certainly
she would find first, and not precisely idling but not
keeping up the morning's smart pace. He wanted to
think about the troy-game.

He was proud of himself for having recognized the
troy, and it irritated him that this had not made their
journey any easier. This was a puzzle he had been set,
and he had solved it before they were half way
through, and it seemed to him that there should be
some reward for his intelligence. The appearance,
perhaps, of the hall of the Order in front of them
today?

No, that was asking too much. Could the journey
not be a little easier from now on? Less of this
laborious use of the bob?

He got it out and sat down, letting it swing idly;
which it did in the direction they had to travel (a lot
of east in it by now). Well, he acknowledged, watching the sun glancing off the worn gold, perhaps he
hadn't solved the puzzle entirely; he had, after all, not

the least idea of the pattern of the centre of the troy. He remembered the circular dint in the entrance stone, and wondered if, long ages gone, that had once been a map of the troy. In times past, perhaps, when the dance was still danced on the eve of spring and the pattern was known freely to everyone?

He blew the dust of his wallet off the brooch and, like Eilian, polished it on his sleeve before he coiled the thong around it. Even Eilian's brooch, treasured by one family, was almost as worn as the entrance stone. He ran his thumbnail round the faint lines where the red colour had been lost, and stared at them suddenly.

Lines going all the length of it; circles, almost, one within the other. He counted them, with difficulty because some of them had disappeared; there seemed to be seven, the right number for a troy. And where they came to the splay there was a pattern, different on each side. A map, a map of the troy?

He picked a blade of grass and tried to trace their path, and then threw it away disappointed. They had begun by going north and turning to the west; the lines on the brooch at that point joined in a kind of flower-shape. It was nothing but an ornament.

And it had delayed him. Another warning, was it, that the troy-game could be played successfully only when abiding by its rules? The sun was sinking, and he did not know where Eilian was.

He set off at a run, thinking in sudden fear that in this broken country it would be easy to lose her. She would have gone on, but without the bob would she keep direction? He scrambled up a bank, and found that he was out of the watery country on to broken grassland, with small groves here and there that broke the sight-lines. They were odd little groves; he did not recognize the trees they were made up of, neat flame-shaped evergreens that had a foolish look of having been planted in groups of five. Then he fell foul of a tangle of briars, and once through those found himself staring into a tree whose upper branches carried three red apples.

Apples! He dropped his bag with Goldeneye and swarmed up after them. They were not easy to reach, but from childhood he had been an expert apple-stealer. He slid down with them stuffed into his tunic, but stopped for a puzzled look. Why were there only three on the branches, and none on the ground?

Then there were more apple-trees, all of them stripped; and then a blank stretch of some strange evergreen which to his astonished eyes seemed to be a hedge. He followed it wondering, and presently came to a break in it. The break had five downward steps leading through it and at each side a stone post. He put a hand to the nearest post, and it tingled in his fingers, briefly and brightly.

He descended the steps and came through the evergreen hedge to the paved walks of an old garden, where on the terrace below a pillared house Eilian was pleasantly sitting and talking to a white-haired man.

Seven

The slanting evening light dazzled him until he could see only dimly as he stalked up the paved way. He was now furiously angry with Eilian. She had left him to worry about her while she sat at her ease. And he was in charge of this journey, not her; what did the girl think she was doing, turning aside from the path to talk to strangers?

She greeted him smilingly. 'You found your way, good. Your Honour, may I present my cousin Brannock king's son of Waymark? Brannock, Justice Ambrosianus.'

She gave him a hard look, a warning that she knew what she was doing in the form of introduction. That meant that their host was at least of equal rank with Brannock. Brannock blinked; he had never heard of a justice, nor of anyone correctly addressed as Your Honour. He summoned his manners, bowed, and murmured that he was happy to meet the Justice.

'And I,' said the Justice, in an accent a little odd but very musical, 'am equally happy to meet the son of so renowned a king. I was about to propose a glass of wine before dinner, but first you would like to wash after your journey. Let me hope that my lazy servants hear me this time.'

He clapped his hands, but Eilian, with the same formal smile, stood up.

'They will be busy about dinner for your unexpected guests, Justice. Let me show my cousin the way.'

'Kind, too kind,' said the Justice. The sun was full on his face, perhaps blinding him, but Brannock had an uneasy feeling that he was not looking quite at either of them. He followed Eilian, noting that the little egg-face was shiningly clean and the marigold-coloured hair in two neat plaits. They went through a pillared entrance and into a paved room like a roofed-in courtyard with doors all round it.

Well, most of it was roofed in. He was dazzled by the sun outside, but thought he could see the sky through rafters in a far corner. He forgot about this in staring at the rest of it; painted walls, a little pool with a marble kerb, and *statues;* he had never seen anything so fine.

Eilian said in a fierce whisper, 'He's very old and he doesn't understand that the servants have gone and the villa's falling down and you're not to tell him; he's very kind.'

'The what's falling down?'

'The villa; this house, that's what he calls it. But he's invited us to eat and sleep here, and he wasn't surprised to see me, except that he said he didn't often have young lady visitors. The way to behave is not to say anything until you're certain what he's talking about.'

Brannock touched one of the pillars, and it tingled so sharply that it stung him. 'If there are no servants,' he said, coming to the most urgent point, 'will there be any dinner?'

'Yes. He seems to think that there are dozens of them, but really there are one old man and his wife. I don't understand them, but they look after him well. Look, come in here.'

62

She took him through a door into two incredible rooms. In the first there was a whole picture on the floor, a great curving green fish of a kind strange to him. When he looked more closely, he saw that it was made up of thousands of tiny squares of coloured stone. Beyond that was something even better: a smaller room with a pool in the middle, with curls of steam rising from the water.

'A bath-house!' he cried, and started to strip off his muddy cloak.

She said reverentially, 'The water's warm and it stays warm; I've never known anything so wonderful. Give me your dirty clothes, I think they'll clean them for you. Have you got another tunic? The Justice dresses as if for a banquet every night, the old servant told me. I know it's hard to leave such a bath, but don't make him wait too long.'

As she had said, it was wonderful. The bath-houses in the village were fed by icy springs, and even cauldrons of boiling water only just took the chill off them. He lolled luxuriously, and then, because Eilian had looked so brushed and neat, spent some time on his own toilet, combing his hair back on his shoulders in the proper way and belatedly blessing his mother for having given him a clean tunic. Because of his caked boots he decided to go barefoot, but found waiting for him in the fish-picture room a wizened, weathered little old man heavily tatooed in blue.

He said, 'Since you are travelling, sir, I fancied you would not have sandals with you, and took the liberty of bringing a pair of my master's.' He indicated one of the stone benches, and knelt and tied them on for him. They were of wonderfully soft leather and gilded round the toe.

Everything else was strange, but Brannock knew

his own world. He looked at the pattern of the tattoos on cheek and arms and said, 'You are from Caledon.'

'I may have been once,' said the old man. 'My name is Niall. It was a long time ago as I see it, and probably best forgotten.'

'And Caledon is a long way away. How did you get here, Niall?'

Niall sat back on his heels and gave him a queer look, half solemn and half satirical. 'The heroes were all done to death, and great songs made over them to be sung to the world's finish, but those of us who weren't heroes had to find a home. It's very snug here, and we give good value in exchange for our refuge.'

'I know little of your heroes in Caledon. What interests me is how you got here. Did you have to come roundabout three times?'

Niall stood up. 'The young lady has taken your other clothes, sir. I will see that they and your boots are cleaned by tomorrow morning. My wife and I were being pursued by a band eager for our death. The hill we fled over was plainly not a hill to be crossed by mortals, but with those behind us we didn't worry about such things. We came down here and found my master in trouble. He was quite alone and nearly gone. So we stayed.'

'What was it that you came past on the hills?'

Niall briefly closed his tattooed eyelids and said, 'Something it is not wise to talk of. Dinner will be served in half an hour, if you will join my master and the young lady on the terrace.'

Eilian and Ambrosianus were in fact below the terrace in the garden, deep in the discussion of herbs. 'Oh basil, you don't know it?' Ambrosianus was saying. 'Your loss, it's quite delicious in any kind of roast dish. Do take a few sprigs with you, it keeps well for a day or so. And there is your noble cousin looking more as he should. Brannock, come and tell me what you think of this wine.'

It was poured from an ordinary earthenware cooling-jug, but Brannock stared at the cups. Two were of horn, but the one given to Eilian was of glass no thicker than a dead leaf. 'My oldest beautiful cup for my youngest beautiful guest!' said Ambrosianus, and mixed the wine half-and-half with water. Eilian took hold of the cup with obvious terror.

'I am no judge of wine,' Brannock said cautiously. 'We get it very rarely.'

'Then you're lucky. I get it not at all. The servants give me native concoctions of honey and herbs, which are tolerably drinkable, and I am thankful that I was always wise enough to keep my cellars well stocked while I could. But it grows chilly – let us see what they have for us for supper.'

They ate in another room off the central hall. There was neither hearth nor brazier, but something mysterious under the floor kept it as warm as a good summer's day. Each of them had a long seat at the side of a low table laden with dishes. Ambrosianus tucked up his feet and lay on his elbow, but waved Brannock down when he would have copied him.

'No no, make yourself comfortable just as you like. I have old-fashioned ways, I know. Eilian my dear, pray observe how my herbs improve a dish. They are skilful with herbs in the kitchen, though a little limited in their ideas now and again.'

Brannock opened his eyes at the word *limited,* for the table seemed to him to be spread lavishly. But as he ate he noticed that the only meat was game-bird, and that most of the dishes were of vegetables and nuts. Goldeneye was given a dish of his own, and Ambrosianus seemed to take pleasure in watching him wolf it down.

'I would so much like to have a dog again,' he said with a sigh. 'My dear old huntress Lysis died untimely, alas, so there were no more litters. Argos was the last of them, and he died – oh, I can't say how many years ago. Here, boy, have this.' Goldeneye accepted most of a dish of game and settled himself to watch Ambrosianus affectionately.

'And now,' he said, refilling their glasses and settling himself in that uncomfortable way on his side and elbow, 'tell me how your journey went. I was surprised to see two young people; I can't remember that happening before.'

'You see other travellers?' Brannock asked cautiously.

'Oh certainly. And fairly regularly. I look forward to the company, living so isolated, and I suspect that they look forward to the respite on what must be a taxing journey. They are elderly, you see. Some sort of a priest, I have always supposed, in a ritual proper to their beliefs, but we have never believed it useful to enquire too closely into such matters.'

Eilian said sudenly, 'You give them supplies when they go on, so that they need not carry too much with them.'

'Naturally. How else should one treat guests? This villa – the marble was imported, of course, and in its early days they called it the Stonesmiths' House – in my great-grandfather's time it was famous for its hospitality to travellers, and you can't expect me to let such a good tradition slip. And from time to time my guests have been kind enough to bring me small gifts in return, seeds and shoots, metal goods the servants

66

don't seem able to find replacements for. You know these priests?'

Eilian had gone very red. 'They sent us on this journey. They should have warned us to bring a gift for you.'

'Now please don't worry about it!' Ambrosianus said comfortably. 'My dear young people, I am used to entertaining as many as ten at a time. You and your excellent dog will hardly strain my resources.'

Brannock thanked him formally. Eilian added the proper form of words, but faintly: she was still deeply embarrassed.

'And since they sent you at an irregular time I shall assume that your people are in trouble. Raiders from the east, I suppose?'

'Do you know about them?' Brannock asked in surprise.

'How could one not know? I have no up-to-date news, of course, but the danger has always been the same. In my day – my earlier days, I mean by that, when – well, dear me, I mustn't go into how long ago that was, but when all one's neighbours kept their villas in good order, an easy hour's ride away, and one could order new books, and give little dinner-parties, and get things properly repaired – even in those happy days you could never be *quite* certain some roving band wouldn't break through from the east. Only after plunder, of course, and the cohort in the town would send them off pretty quickly, but still you'd have to get the men in from the fields and have them stand to arms for the rest of the day, such an irritating upset to their work.'

'They came from the east,' said Brannock, thankfully fixing on the one word he could make sense of.

'But where else? My dear Brannock, this land of ours — and take no notice of my foreign-sounding name, my people have lived here for generations — this land of ours is *rich*. Very much richer than the lands over the eastern seas. Of course it will always attract raiders, and of course it will always be necessary to defend it. In my day we did that pretty well for a long time, though they tell me that things went worse later — but living out here, as I've said, I don't hear the latest news. Now you tell me that they're back. So what have you been sent to do? Call on the people themselves to rise in defence?'

'That is the business of our fathers. We are to ask for help from the Order.'

'Order?'

'We call them elders. The ones you know.'

'I see. That's bad.'

'Is it?'

'Oh, I think so. A last resort, surely? When the military can't handle it, nothing is left but the priests. I'm sorry that there is no more I can do to help than send you on your way tomorrow rested and well-provided. And never lose heart! We fought them off in my time, and you'll do as well now. And now let me call Niall's wife to show you to your rooms, while Niall and I put our heads together over your supplies for the morning.'

He clapped his hands for Niall, and Brannock, remembering his manners, rose and thanked him for the meal. Eilian followed him, but with surprising diffidence added, 'Could I ask you a question, Justice?'

'Anything, my dear.'

'You said your people had been here for generations. So they must have come here from somewhere else.'

'Yes, indeed,' said Ambrosianus heartily, 'and very proud we have always been that we were among the very first of the families to settle here. The civilian families, of course, but long before the land was properly pacified. Oh, we have died in defence against the tribesmen of the hills, I assure you. Now would either of you care for a last drink?'

Eilian went off with Niall's wife, and Niall in his silent fashion took Brannock to yet another room with a magnificent bed and a sheepskin and a bowl of water for Goldeneye. Wishing him good-night, he murmured, 'It is my understanding, sir, that my master's ancestors came from the south; but it was a very long time ago.'

He seemed to think that there was a message in this. Sleepily Brannock thought about it. From the south, and in the wake of an armed invasion. There had been the people who used the arrow-shaped flints and the bone picks; and those who had made and lost the golden brooch; and those who used the delicate glass cups and were called the Stonesmiths. All living in the land, all, perhaps, dying in defence of it; and now his own people. If he had lived a very long time ago, he supposed, he would have fought and died in defence of the land against Ambrosianus's people.

Eight

Looking for everyone in the morning, Brannock found Ambrosianus in the paved garden, playing with a riotous Goldeneye.

'Your young lady cousin,' he, said, reluctantly pushing Goldeneye off, 'is with the servants, choosing the few small items we can give to help you on your way. There, get down now, there's a good dog.'

Brannock, who had spent some thought on this problem, said, 'You will allow us, Justice, on the next visit of our elders, to send you a pair of puppies as a return for your hospitality.'

'Of Goldeneye's line?'

'If you choose.'

'Oh, I do. That is to say — I would, if — well, how shall I put it? I have asked, you see.' There was something absent about Ambrosianus this morning, as if he had become slightly blurred; and he had developed an unnerving way of speaking to Brannock as if he stood curiously far away from him. 'Oh, not for anything of importance, really we do very well here, but for *news*. One's neighbours, you know — of course time goes by so fast, no doubt some of them have died, but it would be pleasant to know. Perhaps I am indeed the very last of us. But no one will bring me news. They are very kind, but as for news it's almost as if I hadn't asked.

But there, I am sure you two young people will do your best, and I shall look forward to my next visitors. And here is Eilian, quite ready, alas, to leave me.'

She was not quite ready, for Niall and his wife had so laden her with food that some of it had to be put into Brannock's bag. When they had had their thanks waved away, she said hopefully, 'We might see you on our way back, Justice.'

'No,' Ambrosianus said, and for once seemed to see them exactly where they were. 'Much as I would enjoy that, my dear, I think not. No one passes the Stonesmiths' House counter-sunwise. But I will hope for your good luck. *Atque in perpetuum, ave atque vale.*'

'And we for yours. What was that last bit?'

'Silly of me! They don't speak the old language now, of course. Hail and farewell, my friends.'

They turned at the gate in the hedge to wave, but Ambrosianus had vanished. Certainly there was much less of the roof intact this morning. Eilian said, as they made their way through the old orchard, 'Perhaps I could send him a cat, too. A queen in kitten, if there was one when the elders were ready.'

'I pity the elder who has to carry her.'

'Yes, perhaps. It was interesting, wasn't it, that no one comes home this way. There must be a different way out of the troy. Come on now, where's your bob? We guessed that we should be going east with some south in it, and all day turning right-handed towards the south. Are we right?'

They were. It looked like being a long day. The weather was slowly worsening, with a light overcast from the east and a chill breeze, and slowly the land was growing more barren, with a yellow stony soil in which little grew but gorse and stunted birch. They stopped at noon in very little shelter, but Niall's wife had put them up some very good bread-cakes that were sweetened with honey, and that made the break pleasant. They discussed their visit to the villa, and Eilian told him with a shiver that she had nearly missed it altogether.

'I was being so careful not to stray from the way, I only looked through the gap in the hedge in case you had gone there.'

'What gap? I didn't see any gap until I came to the stone pillars and steps.'

'What pillars and steps? There was no way in but a ragged gap in the hedge and a muddy slope beyond.'

'Well,' Brannock said ruefully when they had argued this a little, 'I never was sure how much it was there, were you?'

'It varied, I thought. But then I'm not sure how much of this troy is really here. And really where.'

They gave up talking about Ambrosianus after that. They had been given rest and food, and it seemed ungrateful to question it too far. Brannock had another worry on his mind.

'I think we were wrong to separate. We mustn't do it again.'

'I didn't like it,' Eilian acknowledged. 'Going on and on without the help of the bob – Brannock, what happens to those who go the wrong way in the troy?'

Brannock shook his head, meaning not that he did not know but that he did not want to think about it. And there was another side to that thought. If

Eilian were lost in the troy, Brannock would be alone. In decision he pulled over his head the thong that held Mennor's token to the Order.

'In case we lose one another – I don't know if this would help, but there's no reason why only I should carry it.'

He cut the token in two and gave her one half. He did not think it would help, but it was an earnest of her right to it. And he hoped, obscurely, that it would act as a good-luck offering.

It had become so cold by now that they were glad to go on. 'I think,' Brannock said after calculation, 'that this may be the outside circle of the troy. This right-hand curve we're walking is shallower than any yet, don't you think?'

Eilian shaded her eyes from the stiff breeze to squint ahead. 'Shallower and longer. We're going south now, so there's a long way yet.'

They reckoned it was fourteen or fifteen miles from the Stonesmiths' House when the going became painful. The cloud had thickened, bringing on dark long before sunset, the trees had finished and the ground grew thick with stones. Eilian's light weight and shorter stride made this especially difficult, and presently she began to complain about the smell.

'What's the matter with the smell?'

'It's wrong. It's blowing in over that hill to the east, and it's not natural.'

What worried him about the hill to the east was that it had sunk to no more than a long shallow rise. If they strayed from their direction in the bad light it would be too easy to cross it unseeing. 'Try to bear more to your right,' he advised her.

'I *am* trying,' she said crossly, 'because it's all pools of water down here, but every time I want to avoid one I have to sheer off to the left.'

'The smell must be marshes, then. Give me your hand and we'll get on better.'

They struggled on like this for some time, never quite managing to reach the higher ground on their right, but at least keeping on the level. Goldeneye, his eyes slitted and his ears blown awry, followed them miserably.

'We must make camp soon,' Brannock said at last, stopping for a vain look around. 'This is too dangerous in the dark, but we can't spend the night in three inches of water. If we really can't get to higher ground on the right, we might at least find a dry spot if we keep well under the hill on the left.'

'I'm not going left,' said Eilian stubbornly. 'I can't even see the hill, let alone be careful to keep under it.'

Nor, now, could Brannock; nothing but vague glints from the broken pools of water that stretched from around their feet away into darkness. If there was no line of hills to their left, that would explain the strength of the wind that was cracking and whining around them.

But there must be hills to their left! That was the outermost wall of the troy.

He staggered as the wind hurled itself at him, and at the same instant Goldeneye sprang past them with a snarl and attacked something pale that slipped away into the ground and left him bewildered. Brannock called to Eilian, 'Take care!' She turned to him with her arm up to shield her eyes from the wind, and horrified he saw a long gleaming line slide out of the darkness around her feet.

She shrieked, tried to run, and fell flat on her face in an almighty splash of water. The gleaming line shrank and ran silently back into the darkness.

He picked her up dripping and spitting.

'It went for me, it *attacked* me. Don't touch it, Brannock. It isn't natural, it's *salt*.'

Brannock scooped up a handful of water and tasted it, looking out at the eastern darkness where something vaster than he could imagine had replaced the land.

'It's the sea,' he said.

'Then come away from it,' Eilian urged. She wrung out her dripping hem and pulled the skirt higher through her belt. 'Hands again, and backs to the wind until we get out of the water. Never mind the direction, we can pick that up from the bob in the morning. Where's Goldeneye?'

Goldeneye came back shaking his ears, with yellow foam up his flanks. They sent him in front of them to test the depth of the water, and found that it was seldom more than a few inches, and the bottom of firm sand. The water was always flowing, though its directions confused them. They floundered through a quarter-mile of it, Eilian all the time looking vengefully over her shoulder, convinced that the sea was roaring in to attack them. But it seemed to stay in much the same place, and once they were clear of it they found themselves on a rising sandy slope with a few gorse bushes here and there. These were dead or dying, but in this weather that was an advantage. They half-burrowed and half-wrenched out one small bush, and while

Brannock tore himself and his clothes horribly in breaking it up for firewood Eilian and Goldeneye (but particularly Goldeneye) scooped the hole its roots had made into a burrow big enough for three souls and a small fire. They huddled close, ate the first thing they could find in the bags, and fell exhausted asleep.

Nine

Brannock opened his eyes next morning to find himself squinting down at the furring of frost on the blanket under his nose. The storm had left behind a cold sharp day, and the roaring of the sea had sunk to a not unpleasant murmur. He got yawning to his knees to blow up the fire, stood up, stretched, and stared.

Eilian, shaking with cold, crept up behind him clutching the blanket over her cheeks.

'So that's what attacked me last night. It looks innocent now, but don't you trust it.'

'Trust it?' Brannock cried. 'But don't you see what it's done? It's broken into the troy.'

The line of hills that was the outer limit of the troy ran from north-east round to south-east in a long curve, and level with their camp was a crumbling gap of nearly a hundred yards long. Through this the sea was lazily washing back and forth into the salt-marsh that now lay along what they had thought would be their path.

'Then we'd better pass it as quickly as we can,' said Eilian. She turned back to the fire, and was feeding it with the remains of the gorse roots when Brannock rolled over and pushed her head down.

'There's a ship. Beached farther along.'

She raked back the roots and whispered, 'Where's Goldeneye?'

Of course he was not there.

With more confidence than Brannock could feel, she said, 'He'd have warned us if there were men,' and wriggled on her elbows to look over the edge of their burrow. 'Yes, there is a ship,' she said in a pleased way. 'So that's what they look like! I wouldn't trust them either.'

Here Goldeneye descended riotously on them in a flurry of sand, and refused to take an interest in anything but breakfast.

'There may be no one there now,' Brannock admitted, 'but a fire is still dangerous.' Reluctantly they smothered the embers, ate a cold breakfast, and started off. The whole hillside was bare of cover, and all the precaution they could take was to keep on the flank of the sandy hill.

As they walked they saw that the ship had been beached off another break in the wall of the troy. Brannock had no idea how ships were measured, but this one seemed big. It was undecked but for a short space at either end, and had benches for rowers; he counted twenty. The front of it rose high and was carved and painted into the head of a staring animal. The only movement around it was the skein of seabirds shifting and flapping along its side, and Eilian suggested hopefully, 'Perhaps it was wrecked.'

'Perhaps,' said Brannock. He did not believe it, and did not think that she did either. It lay too carefully where the broken hill gave it shelter from the open sea. He got out the bob, and they watched it swing to the south-west.

'Do you think it can feel that that ship's there?' Eilian speculated.

'I don't know. But it doesn't point anywhere near

the ship, and myself I'm not going towards it for anything. Come along.'

Although the day remained cold and sunless, the land improved as they went. First the gorse was alive, and in bloom, and then the grass grew thick and damp, though these scents could not overlay the salt in the air. By mid-morning they were going due west, and could see that ahead the hill was turning sharp right towards the centre of the troy.

'Good; that's away from the sea,' said Eilian. She was not going to forgive it for attacking her. 'And look! – trees again.'

As their hill went round to the north, they could see the beginnings of the familiar sparse forest land of spinneys among bracken.

'Cover,' Brannock said gratefully.

'And fire and food and a proper camp.'

As soon as they met the outliers of this forest they turned uphill into it for the sake of cover. There seemed to be no danger of losing the right path, for even then they were less than half-way up the hill, but Brannock nevertheless had the bob out three times more during the day. They got along fast, chiefly to keep themselves warm, and Brannock grumbled that his clothes had not dried since their soaking in the sea.

'Nor have mine,' said Eilian, suddenly becoming house-wifely, 'and nor they will until they've been washed. Look, thick with salt from that sea.'

'They might be washed too soon,' said Brannock, sniffing the air. He did not understand the weather in these parts, but suspected that there were more storms to come.

'It's queer,' said Eilian some time later, 'how big this forest is. I'm tired to death, but when we first saw it it didn't look more than a couple of miles long. Are you sure we're still on the right way?'

'I'd be happier if we were lower, so that we'd no chance of missing the turn. We can camp once we've found that.'

They bore downhill, and were swinging along at a better pace when Goldeneye stopped dead in the path, the hair rising over his shoulders.

'Down!' Brannock said automatically to all three of them. He crouched to the shelter of a bush, parted the leaves cautiously, and looked down on the turn of the troy.

Across the path they must take a band of men was feasting noisily.

Ten

Eilian at his side was counting under her breath.

'Thirty – upwards of thirty around the fire. Ten or a dozen coming and going, I can't keep count of those. Too many for the crew of one ship, there must be more we haven't seen. That's a sheep they're roasting there. They must have raided some village.'

'Yes,' said Brannock. He felt sick. This was the danger he had been sent to guard against, and he knew now that he had never taken it seriously. He had airily assumed that it would be no worse than the skirmishes among the Seven Kingdoms. One look showed him how wrong he was.

The men were yellow-headed, large-bodied and noisy, and well-armed, though some had piled their helmets and long spears beside the fire. They let their voices boom out over the silent land, in bursts of song and great roars of laughter. One was stabbing the meat to see if it was cooked, two others fooling with wineskins, splashing the wine at one another as they filled cups. They rested at their ease, as if they were conquerors already.

'How did they get into the troy?' Eilian breathed.

'Lean a little this way – do you see? Another gap in the outer hill. The other ships will be beyond there, and this is the rendezvous for the crews. They'll camp here tonight, and tomorrow—'.

Eilian's cold little fingers gripped his. 'We have to get round them. But how?'

They lay a long time watching. The camp lay in the area of level ground where the valley that should be their path went in a broad right-handed sweep round the shoulder on which they lay. On the west it was bounded by a tall white cliff that ran south to north beyond their view. The raiders were setting up a substantial camp, probably to act as a base to store their loot. Half a dozen sheep had been herded into a rough pen, and a big man in a breastplate strolled over to superintend the building of a small lodge of branches. After a time there was a round of cheering as three men rode in from the gap to the south bringing a string of horses with them.

'They're going to send out a mounted patrol,' said Brannock, getting to his knee. But where could they run to?

'I don't think they are,' said Eilian. 'No, look, two of them have dismounted. They were looking over the booty, that's all.'

There were shouts from the fire as two men started carving the meat. The one man still mounted tugged his string to a clump of birches on the outskirts of the camp and got down and began to tether them, shouting over his shoulder to the others.

'They're not even putting out sentries,' Brannock said bitterly; 'they think they're safe. They'll eat and then settle for the night. We must wait.'

'And eat too,' said Eilian, and opened her food-bag. They lay and ate. Presently Eilian said diffidently, 'We couldn't go up over this hill? It's the one way open to us, and we might avoid them and still not actually cross the hill.'

Brannock shook his head, and on the sandy soil

between their elbows drew a plan of the troy. 'Look, we are on the third circle, the outermost one. If we go over this hill, we shall simply come back to where we have been before, the turn from the first circle to the second.'

Eilian puzzled over it. 'I see; the place where we spent the first night. Yes, that way is no good . . . Brannock, what do you think would happen if we did go back to somewhere we've been before?'

'I have no idea,' said Brannock. He spoke curtly, because he had two very good ideas, and did not want to think about either of them. One was that they would then have to make their way back through the troy, the second circle leading to the first and the first to the third and the third back to the second, and so on until they were ghosts and did not know it. The other, of course, was that there would come at them those things it was not wise to speak of. There was even a third, that the troy would at once disappear, and leave them on a bare sea-coast with more invading ships driving in on the wind from the east.

To shake off these thoughts he pulled out the bob. It directed them without hesitation through the raider's camp.

'Well,' said Eilian with a quiver, 'then that's decided. So how?'

It grew darker, but the feasting went on by the light of the fire. More men arrived, in ones and twos or small groups, and were greeted with shouts; most of them carried booty of one kind and another. 'If we were to go like that,' Brannock said, 'we'd be coming from the wrong direction, but perhaps they wouldn't notice that for a few moments.' In the dim twilight he measured the ground by eye. 'I think we shall have to lift two of the horses. I doubt if we can do that without being seen, but at least we should have a start on the pursuit.'

Eilian wriggled the food-bag off her shoulder and passed it to him. 'Then we must loose all the horses and drive them off; that will stop the men riding after us, and confuse them too. You'd better let me do that, I can speak to horses. Take my bag so that I can go softly. The way once we're mounted is round to the right?'

'It looked possible to ride for at least some of the way. You'll be all right so long as you keep on level ground. Don't try to stay together.'

'Then now, while there's still some light.' She was shaking a little, but her voice was composed.

They slid down the hill a yard at a time, whisking from bush to bush and freezing in shelter to watch for signs of discovery.

By now the raiders' band seemed to be complete, and they were gathered around the fire, eating and drinking noisily. There were nine horses, and with the dwarf trees they were tethered to gave fair cover for one. Brannock murmured in Eilian's ear, 'The men can see much less than you can, the fire will dazzle them.' She nodded without looking at him, gave him a push as a signal to wait, and flitted on. Even to him she looked no more than an eddy of the darkness. He held Goldeneye and waited. The horses did not stir, did not seem even to lift a head; but after a moment one of them detached itself from the dark group and wandered in his direction, grazing as it went. He stepped softly to its head and whispered to it. It was a mild beast, round-bellied after the summer, and stood without fuss. Eilian had loosed it without cutting the halter, and he looped it over his arm and watched for the others. At the bonfire there was an angry bellow, and he held the horse close and stroked it for fear of its startling. There were more bellows, then a general shouting, and finally a great roar of laughter. He dared no more than a quick glance, for fear of spoiling his night-sight, but that seemed to have been a drunken quarrel resolved by a joke. Two horses, and then another, strayed out of line, and he heard one blow through his nose in appreciation. Someone at the fire raised his voice again, but this time there was cheering, and several voices began a song. Another horse loose − that was five, and Eilian was more than half-way. Then suddenly all of them were loose, and Eilian was mounted, and not riding away but in the middle of them, turning her horse wildly and shrieking, 'Hup, hup!' And mingled with her shrieks was a man's shouts.

There had been a sentry with them all the time, and she had almost done her work without alarming him. Brannock vaulted on his mount, struggling with the burden of two food-bags, shouted to Goldeneye, and rode down on the guard, screeching to the horses. They scattered widely, both from him and from the outburst from around the fire. He had an instant's glimpse of figures running towards them, and then came suddenly on the sentry and Eilian. He had one handful of mane and another of Eilian's arm and was fighting to get a foothold; she was lying askew on her horse's neck, half-dragged off, kicking frantically to keep it going. Brannock pulled his horse savagely round, got out his long knife and cut the sentry across the back. He fell away with a yell, and Eilian vanished, swept away into the darkness. Brannock shouted after her, 'Go on!' and wheeled to make the turn at speed between her and the raiders.

No danger from them now! They were streaming

away from the fire, shouting and clashing their weapons, but without horses that was all they were good for. Brannock eased to a trot for a space, to be sure none had contrived to recapture a horse, and then turned his horse's head north and kicked him on.

There was a hiss in his ear. Something clapped him stunningly over the shoulder and whipped past his horse's neck. He saw a cut lock of mane fly behind him. The horse squealed with pain, threw up its head, and plunged wildly. The halter snapped. One of the food-bags fell away. Thrown on its neck, one arm useless, Brannock was carried by a bolting horse the wrong way into the troy.

Eleven

For some time Goldeneye had been wandering around and sighing. Now he put a heavy paw on Brannock's side and forced him to admit that he was awake.

He uncurled himself, sat up, and put his head between his hands and wondered how to face the day.

What kind of a day it was he could hardly tell, for little light and no sunshine penetrated the trees far above his head. This was the ancient deep forest; not the mild open kind that could be travelled with little trouble, but the oldest oak forest, where men never went, where the vast trees grew and died and toppled and rotted untouched, as they had done since the beginning of the world. His one shoulder was swollen and immovable from where the spear butt had hit it before it grazed his horse's neck, and the rest of him cut and bruised and shaken from the stunning fall he had taken when the terrified beast had crashed to the crest of some hill and his hold had at last loosened. He had come off forwards, rolled downhill, and never found his way back. He had not expected to. He had taken the wrong way in the troy, and from that there was no turning back.

He had lost his horse; he had lost his long knife and one food-bag. And he had lost Eilian, and Eilian had ridden off with no food and no guide. And the raiders were here, victorious and in force. When he came to feel timidly for his bob, he found that his wallet had been torn open and the bob had fallen out.

He told Goldeneye to leave him alone. After a long time he heard a sound and looked up. Goldeneye was cheerfully eating something furry.

'You could have learned that lesson earlier,' he said sourly.

Goldeneye smacked his chops, grinned, and vanished. Presently he came back with his tail waving and his muzzle dripping.

'You could at least show me where it is,' Brannock said angrily. He was not hungry, but his thirst was enormous. Goldeneye jumped obligingly through undergrowth that seemed to be rooted in rotting wood, over a head-high fallen trunk grown over with crimson and purple fungus, and stopped where a trickle under the leaves had collected into a string of tiny brown pools. Brannock drank deeply, splashed his face, washed his cuts, shook out his boots and ate some bread. That made him feel a little better, but no less lost.

He held his aching head again and thought about Eilian. She would have got safely into the fourth circle. She knew she had to go counter-sunwise and that her way lay between the surrounding hills. So far she would be safe, and if she found water she could last for a time on nuts and berries. But what would happen to her at the end of the fourth circle?

She would make guesses; and because she was Eilian her guesses would be sensible and practical. But it had become only too plain that good sense was not enough to take you through a troy, and she had not the gift of working the bob.

He wondered, purely in a spirit of dismal enquiry, what his bob would have said to him now.

Well, Mennor had said that there was value in the gold buckle, but that was not by any means his first bob. All he needed was a thread and something to weight it with. If it was worth the trouble.

He did not think that it was worth the trouble. All he felt, in fact, was a profound anger at having wasted so much effort to fail at the last. Having wasted, he acknowledged, Eilian's final brilliant effort in loosing the horses unseen. He put his fingers forlornly into his torn wallet to see if there was anything there that would serve as a weight, and tucked into a bottom corner found something oddly familiar.

Pleasantly familiar. In his fingers was the holed pebble that he had discarded when Mennor gave him the buckle. He had had the pebble for years, and he remembered that it was of the kind that his mother called an oracle-stone.

He unravelled some threads from the edge of his blanket, made three three-way plaits and then plaited them together. He had no idea why this seemed to be the right way to do it, but Eilian's words about the value of setting charms rightly were in his mind, and he went about it carefully, knotting the top of the final nine-way plait, trimming the end with his eating-knife, threading it through the hole in the stone and knotting and trimming again.

The first thing he felt as he held out the completed bob was that it hung well, firm and weighty. But before it could start to swing he caught it in a hurry into his palm and sat for a time in thought. He had used his bob carelessly often enough; for once let him use it as it deserved of him.

And it was surprising, he came ruefully to find, how simple things were when you spent some thought on them. He understood a great deal now, and he fancied that he might have understood most of it long before now if he had ever tried. They had been wrong, wholly wrong about straying out of their way in the troy; though entirely right to think that it would be disastrous to do so. No terrifying phantoms would have come at them if they had ever gone over the hill; all that would have happened was that having willingly given up the way they would never have found it again. The terrifying phantom at the beginning of the journey? Well, it might have been a not-unfriendly warning of what he must understand, but he thought it much more likely to have been a private terror of his own, telling what he had secretly known all the time, that to succeed in his errand he must not look for easy ways round.

So that was one fear the less on Eilian's behalf. That was why he was here, unharmed, only having lost his way, and with it his chance of ever coming to the centre of the troy.

Unless, unless! He held the bob in his cupped hands. He had the favour of the land. He knew that now better than ever before; this ancient forest was as friendly to him as his own village fields. If it was only to find Eilian, he would follow his bob wherever it took him; he would not believe that he had lost its favour now.

He opened his hands and let the bob swing.

It hung heavy for an instant and then gave him a brisk direction: a point to the west of north, and directly downhill.

'Thank you,' he said, and put it carefully away and stood up to see how he must go.

He must go, he saw, in the only possible way. The trickle of water went downhill, and trickles if followed become rivulets and rivulets streams, and where water went there must be a way for him. He called Goldeneye and began to slide and scramble and crash his way a point to the west of north. And as he went he worried unceasingly about Eilian. Had she found anything to eat?

They slept that night in acute discomfort on the only square yard of level ground they had seen all day, but by then the rivulet was all of a foot wide and flowing easily. In the morning there was sunlight; not very much, and still only filtering hazily through the leaves far above, and the descent below seemed a little less steep. After an hour or so he found a pool big enough to bathe in, though briefly, for it was icy cold. He shook the mud and twigs from his clothes, combed his wet hair back with his fingers and repinned his cloak with attention to the proper folds. He could not brush away the thick white stains that crusted its hem; they were salt from the sea, which seemed an age and a world away. He thought that Eilian must be very hungry now, and set off at a good pace down the slope of the sun-dappled forest.

It was past noon before the trees thinned out, and soon after that the land ran level for a time, and then rose through gentle pastures to a grassy knoll standing in a shallow cup between two low hills. Even without what stood on the top of the knoll it looked like an entrance; but on the knoll, very black against the bright sky, were two standing stones with a third across the top: an ancient dolmen.

But no Eilian? Disappointed, he felt for the bob, and then took his hand away. His direction was marked for him up there.

He climbed the knoll, looking every moment for Eilian, and the view from the top opened upon him.

The hills on the left and right, quite bare and green, ran in a perfect ring a quarter of a mile across. In the middle of it was a circle of thirteen pairs of standing stones, each with a third across the top. He was at the centre of the troy.

His first sensible thought was that this was wrong. He had not followed the way of the troy, so he could not have arrived at its centre.

Then he saw that he was not yet at the centre, but still outside the entrance, and that he was not alone. In front of the entrance dolmen was a broad threshold stone, and on it a figure was sitting.

'Eilian!' he called, and ran. In some way she had come the way of the troy, and he was allowed to join her.

The figure stood up. It was not Eilian. He stopped in deep disappointment.

It was a man; young, perhaps two or three years older than Brannock, and decidedly a splendid figure. His long curling hair was lighter than his brown smiling face, his tunic and boot-tops were embroidered and his belt and knife-sheath studded with gold. On the stone at his side were a jug, two cups, and a platter of silver.

He held out his hand. 'Brannock king's son, welcome! And bravely travelled. But where is Eilian king's daughter? We expected her as well.'

These were ceremonial manners, Brannock thought confusedly, and one did not burst into them with a torrent of questions. He said haltingly – it seemed a long time since he had spoken to anyone but Goldeneye or the bob – 'Thank you for your welcome, and I am happy to see you. I was parted from Eilian. I am anxious for her safety. Who are you, sir?'

'I am Ansgar earl's son.' From somewhere south, Brannock judged by his accent. 'And please don't worry about Eilian. We will see to it that she comes to no harm. Won't you take some refreshment? Oh, and this is your handsome Goldeneye. Good dog, then; come and share with us.'

Goldeneye, Brannock was glad to see, was on his ceremonial manners too. He did not throw himself enthusiastically on Ansgar, but stayed loftily at heel and pretended not to see the bread on the platter. Brannock would have liked to ask how Ansgar could be certain that Eilian was safe, but that could not politely be done until the refreshment was dealt with. He sat down and accepted a cup.

It was splendidly chased with twining patterns, and it held wine. Ansgar laughed at his sigh of pleasure.

'Good wine after a journey, is there anything better?'

'You are more fortunate than us,' Brannock returned politely. 'We get very little wine these days.'

'Oh, we have our sources of supply,' Ansgar said. For some reason this seemed to amuse him. 'Let me give you bread with it.'

He passed over the platter, and Brannock reached into his wallet for his eating-knife. Somehow the thread of the bob had wound itself round the handle, and Ansgar said very softly, 'Ah!' and leaned forward to look. Brannock disentangled the knife and cut his own slice and a corner for Goldeneye, which he tossed to him for fear he should disgrace them both by begging. Goldeneye caught it, dropped it between his paws, and looked steadily into the distance.

Ansgar said swiftly, 'A capable dog, I see, who has already hunted for himself.' He leaned over to refill Brannock's cup. Brannock was covertly admiring his

93

clothes, though noting on a nearer view that the splendour was stained by wear. Through the embroidery ran crusted white lines, and he remembered ruefully trying in vain to rub just such lines off his own cloak this morning.

For some reason this brought Eilian even more urgently into his mind.

'And that,' said Ansgar, 'is the famous instrument of your divining. They tell me that you are more masterful with it than any man known.'

Brannock began, 'Masterful is wrong. You do not have mastery over—' and met Ansgar's eye. His smile was friendly, but his eye was calculating.

Brannock put down the bread and wine. Ansgar was flattering him, and he had a reason for it. Ansgar wanted the use of the bob, and he wanted it for his own purposes, not the land's. To take bread and wine from a man, Brannock remembered, was to acknowledge yourself his guest and friend. And suddenly in his memory he heard Eilian's voice, in one of her irritating housewifely moods. Their clothes, she declared, would not dry because of the salt in them. Salt was the white stain on his own cloak, and Ansgar's clothes were white with it. Ansgar had come by sea.

And, what was worse, Ansgar had arrived here knowing about Eilian, and their journey, and Goldeneye, and the bob.

Brannock took the bread from between Goldeneye's paws and tossed it away, and got wearily to his feet. Not even on the morning after losing Eilian had he felt so despairing. He had come against all hope to the centre of the troy and found there nothing but the enemy from the east.

*　*　*

94

Ansgar too stood up; but quietly, and with his face much improved without the flattery. 'Probably better to have told you the truth at once,' he said thoughtfully. 'Let me explain matters. First of all, don't worry about Eilian. There's a mounted party out searching for her, but they have strict orders to treat her as a friend. Yes, we weren't very friendly the other night down by the sea, but how were we to know who you were? All we saw were two horse-thieves.'

It did not seem worth mentioning that Ansgar's men had stolen the horses first. Brannock found a spark of comfort in Goldeneye's cold nose touching his hand.

'If we had known whose son you are — whose daughter Eilian is—'

Goldeneye's nose again. Brannock looked down at him. He had his head turned to stare at the dolmen.

This was not the centre of the troy. The centre was through the dolmen.

Brannock stopped looking at Goldeneye and said at random, 'What have my father and uncle to do with this?'

'Your two most powerful kings,' said Ansgar earnestly, 'and ourselves, why should we quarrel when our interests are the same? Do you take us for common raiders, in and out between tides for the sake of a little loot? We are *not*; we are settlers, we come in peace but in strength, we want to share the land with you.'

Something had moved in the corner of Brannock's vision. He dared a brief glance at the dolmen, and felt Goldeneye against his knee shiver with excitement.

Under the stone arch, half in and half out of the light of the declining sun, a tall old man was standing, watching them unconcernedly.

'So what is the obvious course?' said Ansgar, 'Your

father and his brother join forces with us, between us we drive out these five petty kings who have always caused so much trouble—'

Brannock interrrupted, 'My father would never act treacherously to our own people!'

'My dear Brannock,' Ansgar said kindly, 'what an extraordinary idea, of course your father isn't treacherous! We have the greatest faith in his loyalty. Who do you think told us that you and Eilian had gone off on some silly errand, and begged us to find you and take you home? And your uncle Rhodri too, of course; and Illtud, who has been friendly for some time with my cousin Petrock, who has been over here preparing the way for this alliance. Oh, and your father asked me to give you this, just in case you misjudge us.'

With a slight flourish he handed over a written token.

Brannock looked at it for some time, hoping to find a sign that it was not what it seemed. But in vain; there was no mistaking his father's ham-fisted way with runes.

'And you,' finished Ansgar with a broad smile, 'are essential to the success of our enterprise. The man who can find secret paths, weapon-hoards, buried treasures—'

Brannock said, 'There's only one thing I don't understand.'

'Tell me!'

'How did you find your way here?'

'What was the difficulty?' said Ansgar in surprise. 'We saw the line you took from the shore the other night. I watched for you here because there's a view all round.'

Brannock asked, 'And the dolmen?' and turned to

look at it. The tall old man was watching them placidly.

'What dolmen?' said Ansgar.

Brannock dropped his father's token on the ground and broke it under his heel. When he looked back at the tall old man, he saw that he had lifted one beckoning finger.

Ansgar was not as ingenuous as he had been making out. One hand whipped out his long knife, the other took Brannock hard by the elbow, and he shouted over his shoulder. There were answering shouts and half a dozen armed men came pounding up the knoll. Goldeneye uttered an extraordinary noise, a kind of snarling yell, and with a leap fastened his teeth in Ansgar's knife arm, hanging with all four feet off the ground. Stumbling free, Brannock looked wildly for the tall old man. He did not appear to have moved, his finger still calmly crooked, but he seemed oddly grey and blurred.

Everything, in fact, looked grey and blurred. The top of the knoll was full of armed men, stumbling, swearing, beating with their hands at a swirling mist that was blowing around them. Brannock broke between them, shouted for Goldeneye, and bolted towards the dolmen. He ran into it so fast that he clapped up against the stone. There was at once a dead silence.

He recovered some breath and turned to the old man. On the farther side of the dolmen the autumn sun shone slanting on the stone circle; on the hither side was a wall of mist. The old man touched his lips for silence and nodded him on. Brannock bowed to him in thanks and ran on out into the sunlight and over the short grass to the centre of the troy.

97

Twelve

He halted at the entrance to the stone circle; and nothing happened.

He called despairingly, 'Eilian!'; and no one answered.

The shadows of the stone stretched far into the east, and in the cold sky the stars were pricking through. There was no sound, no movement, and yet he was not alone. Somewhere near him he knew there was an intense busyness beyond the reach of his senses.

It was not beyond the reach of Goldeneye's. His ears were pricking, and his eyes following something inside the stone circle. All Brannock could see there was the ring of turf. He put his hands for comfort on the warm surface of the nearest stone, and it tingled softly to him and a man came round the side of it, smiling. 'Brannock king's son,' he said, 'welcome.'

He was young and slender and wiry, with tight curls of black hair, and he wore the robe of an elder, but kilted high through his belt. 'I am Teithi,' he said, and held out his hand. 'How can we help you?'

'I think you have,' said Brannock. 'Is it safe in here?'

'Perfectly. The rowdy lot beyond the dolmen will see nothing of interest and go away. Were you looking for the hall of the Order?'

'No,' said Brannock. He was grateful to find that about this his mind was quite clear. 'I lost that way three nights ago. I am looking for one who is coming through the troy. Have you news of Eilian king's daughter?'

'*Eilian* is coming through the troy?' said Teithi, and looked perplexed. 'Well; yes, I believe there may be news of her. There was a horse found straying yesterday. No, no! You need not be afraid. He had been turned loose, for he wore a halter that had been knotted on his neck. And the inner circles of the troy are too steep to be ridden. But I see that you have had a hard journey lately; you need a meal and a bed.'

'Thank you, but no. Eilian has no guide through the troy, and I must find her.'

Teithi stared at him aghast. 'But no one travels the troy the wrong way!'

'No, well, so I've heard,' said Brannock. 'But I've never actually done it, so I must try now.'

Teithi hurriedly took his arm. 'Please! We can't – I do advise you against it. At least until the morning!'

His round good-natured face was earnest, but it seemed to Brannock that what he had been going to say was *We can't allow it*. He said after a moment, 'It's bad travelling in the dark. Thank you for your offer, and I would be grateful for a night's rest.'

'There's sensible!' said Teithi, beaming in relief, and took him sunwise half-way round the stone to a solitary hut that had certainly not been there before. Not *visibly* there, for the fire-bed was full of warm ashes. There was bread and cold meat set ready, and Teithi sat down to eat with him. To keep

99

a watch on him, Brannock thought, but could not help warming to his good nature and his honest concern about Eilian.

'You were separated by the easterners, but you think she rode in the right direction.' He shook his head. 'The troy is *intended* to stop those who attempt it without a guide, and it doesn't get easier the farther you go. I wouldn't attempt it alone myself.'

'You? Aren't you an elder?'

'Not for years yet; a student only, and when I take the troy it's with a full elder, and they carry the pattern in their heads. I'll tell you what I suspect, though, and you're never to say I told you.' They were growing friendly over the good meal in the warm hut. 'I've seen elders themselves at sea in the troy.'

'You said they carried the pattern—'

'Oh, the *pattern's* always the same. It's the land itself that changes. You know you've a right-handed turn to make, but when you look for a landmark that was there last time it's gone, and it's something entirely different that's taken its place.'

'Yes,' Brannock said, regarding him thoughtfully, 'Mennor said something of the kind. That the troy was a secret of the land itself. So it's not under the control of the Order?'

'Not a bit. Those who pretend to know about it say that the troy is here to protect the hall of the Order. Don't you believe it! The troy isn't here because of the Order, it's the other way round; the Order built their hall here because of the troy.'

'The troy has its own ways,' said Brannock nodding; and then stopped looking thoughtful and changed the subject.

They finished their meal and bedded down. The beds were well supplied with skins and more comfortable than any he had slept on since the night at the Stonesmiths' House, and it was difficult not to fall asleep; but he lay with one hand on Goldeneye and struggled with his treacherous eyelids until he had beaten them into wakefulness and Teithi's breathing on the other side of the hut was faint and peaceful. Then he slid from beneath the covers, seized Goldeneye with one hand and his boots with the other and crept outside.

There was no moon, but the stars were piercingly bright on the rime that lay everywhere. Pulling on his boots, he took a very sharp look at the stone circle. It wavered a little and then steadied, which was very much what he might have expected. He got out his bob and let it swing. It directed him to the entrance dolmen. And that too was as might have been expected.

He had been counting as he lay in the hut. The first circle had been sunwise, so the seventh and last would also be sunwise. He came out of the dolmen and turned counter-sunwise.

At once Goldeneye stiffened, stalked forward, and screamed. It was a scream such as Brannock had never heard from him before. He hurled himself forward and came on him hunched, whirling, trying to shake off something fastened on his back. Brannock flung himself upon him, hit out wildly, and felt claws rake his cheek and hands. Goldeneye rolled free and bolted, yelping. Something red-eyed in the darkness faced Brannock growling. On the ground between them lay something limp and furry.

It was a dead coney.

'Pangur!' cried Brannock, 'Oh Pangur, Pangur, *Pangur*!' and swept him up and hugged him, and was scratched again for it. Eilian came limping up the slope and said, 'Goldeneye wasn't trying to steal your coney. Do call him back, Brannock, and make sure he hasn't been hurt.'

'You got here,' said Brannock, and for a time could say no more. 'I was starting out to find you. You're all right, not harmed?'

'I'm all right. It was just rather a long way. It was Pangur and the Bach Bychan who did most of it. If this is where we were coming, where is it? And how did you get here?'

'And how did you? And who is the Bach Bychan? Yes, this is the centre of the troy, but I think it's charmed against me because I didn't come the right way, and there's news I have for you, not good I'm afraid, but now you've arrived—'

It was, of course, Eilian who insisted that they sit down and tell their stories properly. She took Pangur, and Brannock the coney, and they tucked themselves in shelter under the arch of the dolmen, and presently a shaken Goldeneye joined them, keeping well away from Pangur, and Eilian refused to say a word until she knew if the Bach Bychan had been found.

'Oh, your horse!' Of course, Brannock thought, she would have to give him a fond name. 'Yes, he's been found, yesterday I think, and he's here. You rode part of the way?'

Of course again, she could not be stopped from praising her horse and her cat. Never, she insisted, had there been such a kind, strong and intelligent horse as the Bychan. How he had kept his footing in the wild scramble away from the invaders' camp, with

102

her hanging half off his neck, she would never understand; nor how he had gone on so surely in the darkness, carrying her into the fourth circle safe from pursuit.

'And then I waited for you until daylight, and I couldn't stay there, we had decided that there was no going back in the troy, so I had to go on.' She looked at him a little anxiously, but he nodded. 'I thought all that day that you might catch me up, because the land was very broken and we kept making detours, but there was grazing for the Bychan and I rode as long as I could. There was water for us both, and I found some nuts, but not many, and by the time night came I'd had to lead him for two hours and knew I'd have to turn him loose. Well, I did feel a bit lost that evening. But when I woke up in the morning,' she said with admiration, 'there was Pangur asleep on my feet and a fish lying ready for me to cook for breakfast.'

'But you said,' Brannock objected, 'that he couldn't come with us because it was too far for a cat to travel.'

'Yes, but the Bach Bychan had taken me so far that I was back at the west side of the troy. The clever cat had only had to cross the hills in between. And he rode on my shoulder after that and when we camped he hunted for us both.'

Brannock said proudly, 'Goldeneye hunted too. I'll tell you about that later. Go on.'

'Oh. Well, that's about all.'

'Of course it isn't! You had three more circles to travel.'

'Yes. Well, they were quite short. And just as you guessed, sunwise and counter and sunwise again. Tell me what happened to you.'

Why she had no wish to talk about the last three circles he could not make out, but he was so glad to have found her that he was even willing to let her have her own way; at least for a time. He recounted his journey through the ancient forest, and then discovered that he had no wish to talk about his adventure with Ansgar. He was able to avoid it for a time, for she was curiously interested in his making of a new bob.

'Yes, but how did you lose the old one?'

'I told you, my wallet was torn open.'

'But you had the holed stone. And your knife.'

'Yes, that was lucky. And so I came here; and listen, I said there was some bad news I had to tell you. I'm sorry, and I hope it will turn out that it isn't true, but—'

Eilian said detachedly, 'Oh, it's true all right. How else do you think I knew the Bychan's name?'

'The *Bychan*? What has he to do with your father?'

'He belonged to him, of course. I recognized him when I was cutting them loose. And he wasn't stolen, because the sentry with them, the one you cut down and I hope you *hurt* him, was one of our grooms. There's no shirking it, Brannock; both our fathers have gone over to the enemy. I blame Illtud.'

'Yes,' said Brannock, so relieved that she was not more distressed that he could regard it himself more composedly; 'Ansgar knew him well, he said. And there was a man called Petrock who is his cousin.' He told her about Ansgar, and to his pleasure she commended his noticing of the salt on his cloak. 'And then there was this elder standing in the dolmen here, and he charmed up a mist and I got away.'

'Into *there*?' She cast a slightly nervous look over her shoulder. 'That's the centre of the troy – the place we've been looking for all this time? What is it, then?'

'I don't know. Nothing to me, because I didn't come through the troy. There's a stone circle, and no one but a nice student called Teithi. I think we shall see it now that you're here.'

'Oh. Then we'd better go in, hadn't we?'

She drew a deep breath and stood up. Brannock pulled her down again.

'Not yet. I want an explanation first.'

She said, 'Oh,' again in a flurried way. 'You want to know how I found my way through the troy without a bob. Yes, well; I didn't want to tell you because it would make you so cross.'

'Me cross? Why?'

She said simply, 'Because I found it when you didn't.'

He had been honestly glad to find her again, but this was very hard to bear. It was a time before he could say, 'I won't I promise I won't. What was it you found?'

She undid the brooch from her shoulder and gave it to him in silence.

'But I did think of it! I looked at it – at mine – I looked carefully, that afternoon before we came to the Stonesmiths' House. And it didn't show the way, it *didn't*! Look—' He took her out into the starlight and traced the delicate twinings of the brooch's ornaments in the splay. 'Look! We went in at the entrance and turned left. These lines have no entrance!'

'It is so very simple,' she said. 'The lines don't mark the paths. They mark the barriers.' She added consolingly, 'You didn't need to understand, because you had the bob.'

'I may have had the bob,' he said wholeheartedly, 'but it didn't stop me being stupid. Come on; we'll go into the centre of the troy.'

And they went through the arch of the dolmen, and saw the lights shining through the windows of the hall within the stone circle.

Thirteen

It was a good-sized substantial hall facing south, with store-houses and stables and grain-pits, and servants were drawing water and feeding hens and splitting kindling. Teithi came to meet them, giving Brannock only one brief glance of reproach before he greeted Eilian.

'Eilian king's daughter, welcome to Caerdroia!'

Eilian, predictably, said, 'Thank you, and this is my cat Pangur who needs a place to sleep, and I would like to visit my horse the Bach Bychan.'

Teithi blinked a little, beginning, 'The chief of the Order—' and then began again. 'Your horse has been cared for, and so shall your cat be. If you will come this way—'

He called a man passing with a load of newly baked bread, and Eilian went off with him, Pangur riding on her shoulder. Returning to Brannock with a suppressed grin, he added, 'She says she's not going to present herself to any chief with her hair full of burrs. You also are not very tidy, Brannock. Can I lend you a clean tunic?'

They went to the bath-house (which was bitterly cold and reminded Brannock sadly of the Stonesmiths' House), and Brannock apologized for leaving secretly.

Teithi gave him an acute glance and said, 'You aren't in the least repentant. You only say that because you suspect that I have been blamed for it. Well, I was told to keep you under my eye, but only because we didn't understand what was happening to the troy. We have never before known anyone arrive here without following its path.'

'But I didn't,' Brannock objected. 'I couldn't see the hall.'

'True; but if you had merely strayed here, like that young easterner, you would have seen nothing but a good viewpoint; no dolmen, no ring of hills, nothing but a barren waste. Nor is it very likely that you would even have strayed *here*. The bob gave you a direction, you said; otherwise, I think, you would still have been wandering in the ancient forest. Yes, this tunic will fit, though I haven't your height . . . Did he say anything else about their purposes hereabouts?'

'Ansgar?' said Brannock from inside the tunic. He did not care to talk about Ansgar, partly because of the faint shameful memory that he had begun to like him. 'Only that they were searching for Eilian, a mounted party. Why?'

Teithi looked dissatisfied. 'We have news of more than one mounted party, who are very urgent about their search. It seems possible that it is not only Eilian they want.'

He refused to say more than that, and began to show signs of nervousness and hint that the chief of the Order was not to be kept waiting too long. They left the bath-house and found Eilian, scrubbed and neat. She said, 'The Bychan is very well and Pangur is asleep in his hay-rack, and here is the other half of your token.'

She took it from her wallet, and Brannock slipped his over his head and gave it to her. 'Yours now, not

108

mine,' he said. Teithi led them into the hall of the Order.

It was the usual sort of hall, with the hearth down the middle, sleeping benches along the walls, and the high chair on a dais in the centre of the long wall, and the usual sort of morning activity was going on in it, servants building up the fire and bringing in platters and jugs for breakfast, and a good score of elders eating, talking, or simply turning to stare; the buzz of conversation almost stopped as Eilian and Brannock entered. But it was full of marvellous things, and, remembering Mennor's hut, Brannock understood now that they were things that had once belonged to the men long dead who had lived in the land. True, few of them were perfect, but there were so many that what was missing in one was there in another. There were arrows with tanged flint tips held on with pine-tree gum, and bone picks set in wooden handles polished with long use, the shoulder-blades of unknown animals etched with pictures of those animals, flowered tiles such as had been laid in the floors of the Stonesmiths' House, a whole tree-branch hung with strung necklaces of blue and gold and blood-colour, and fine glass, a great deal of fine glass, but none of it whole like the cup Ambrosianus had filled with wine for Eilian. But the most precious of all were kept around the high chair, and they were matter for reading: runes on every imaginable material, from stone tablet to a long sword with a jewelled gold hilt.

The man in the high chair said, 'I am Maldwyn. Have you a token for me?'

He was the stillest man Brannock had ever seen. He sat with his head resting on the back of the chair and his hands resting on the arms, and the liveliest thing about him was his eyelids. To be chief of the Order he must be old, but he looked no more than reasonably, even fiercely, mature. Though the elders had come crowding around the high chair, no one spoke, and Teithi was visibly nervous of him.

Eilian gave him her well-brought-up bow and offered him the token, saying, 'This is from both of us.'

Teithi took it from her in a hurry and put it into Maldwyn's hand. Maldwyn ran his thumb over it without looking at it, and said, 'Tell me who sent it, and why.'

Eilian turned to Brannock, who said, 'It was sent by Mennor, the elder from my – from Hywel's kingdom of Waymark. His word to me was that this invasion from the east was more dangerous than ever before.'

Maldwyn nodded, very gently, once. As if this were permission to speak, the surrounding elders began a buzz of agreement, and one nodded familiarly to Brannock and said, 'As this young man knows better than most.'

Brannock recognized him as the tall old man who had summoned up the mist that had rescued him from Ansgar, and said to him, 'Thank you for your help.'

'Scilti,' the tall old man introduced himself.

'And he said,' Brannock went on to Maldwyn, 'that the token cast his vote for a final course of action.'

The buzz of agreement stopped at once.

Maldwyn did not exactly look shocked, but he gave Brannock a long sharp glance, and at last looked down at the token in his palm. His eyebrows went up and his lips tightened. 'Final,' he said as if to himself.

The buzz began again, and that did sound shocked. Brannock finished, 'He said it was an action that

110

you would not embark on without the consent of each one of the Order.'

'Ah,' Maldwyn said softly; and that was all.

Brannock could not have said what he had expected from his announcement, but it was not this. He shot a glance at Eilian, and saw that she was watching Maldwyn under her brows, with her lip caught hard in her teeth.

Scilti said thoughtfully, 'Mennor was always a politician.'

Maldwyn said to Brannock, 'You and your cousin have discovered or guessed at much of the politics behind this.'

'Oh. Yes,' Brannock said reluctantly. 'There was a man, Petrock, who was a guest of my father's the day I left. I believe he had also been a guest of Eilian's father.' He looked at her, and she nodded briefly. 'The easterner Ansgar told me that he was his cousin. When we took the horses from the easterner's camp, my cousin saw that they were guarded by a groom of her father's. Ansgar told me that the Eastmark elder Illtud was his friend, and that our – that the kings Hywel and Rhodri had agreed to support their invasion in return for the easterner's help in defeating the other five of the Seven Kings.' Since it had to be said, he added, 'I do not support my father in this.'

'Nor I mine,' said Eilian with a snap.

Scilti nodded to Brannock and said, 'Never for a moment did I think you would. But believe me, you would have had no helpful mist if you had acted otherwise.'

There was a great deal of murmuring going on among the elders. Brannock tried to hear too much of it at once, and became confused. He looked at Eilian, and thought she had understood better, for she had

111

gone greenish-white and pinched in the face. Maldwyn surprised him by saying, 'There are things we do not understand about your journey. The troy is a very old secret we did not think could be penetrated but by those to whom the key was passed down.'

It seemed to Brannock that the time for talk about the troy was passed, but he said as civilly as possible, 'I didn't penetrate it, but my cousin did.'

He looked at Eilian, who said curtly, 'As the elder daughter of my mother's family I carry a very ancient brooch with the pattern of the troy on it.'

She did not offer to show the brooch, and Maldwyn, after a long look at her, did not ask to see it, but turned his eyes to Brannock.

'But you went out of the right path and yet arrived here. This is what we do not understand.'

'Nor do I,' said Brannock, meaning, did it matter now? But as Maldwyn waited for him to go on, and the elders had stopped murmuring among themselves, he began, 'When I found myself in the ancient forest, my bob—'

'We do not understand the power of the bob,' Maldwyn interrupted him.

Eilian said in a burst of impatience, 'Show them, Brannock.' She turned to him and took hold of his wallet, so that she could breathe into his ear, 'They're *jealous*.'

She was right, Brannock realized as he got out his bob. She was angry about it, but he was not; partly because he understood their feelings, finding an untutored boy wiser than they were after all their years of study; and partly because he understood the workings of the bob rather less than they did. He nodded at her not to worry, and wound the thong of

112

the bob round his finger and moved clear of her so that the elders could see him.

'It comes, I think,' he said, 'from the favour of the land, which is given at birth and at random, needing neither intelligence nor study to employ it. I have heard of its being used to find water in dry places; I can find metals, and things that are lost, and it was only Mennor who taught me that I could use it to find a secret path. There is no art in it but to let the bob hang free, so, and watch how it—'

He came to a stop. Slow but decided, the bob was beginning to swing.

'Eilian!' he said. She was at his side, watching. They had both forgotten the elders and Maldwyn.

'South,' she said, 'due south. What does that mean?'

'Quickly,' he said.

Side by side they ran out of the hall and south towards the dolmen entrance.

Through it a figure was striding.

'Mennor!' shouted Brannock.

'Good!' breathed Eilian.

Fourteen

He was in a towering rage.

'Hunted,' he said, 'hunted in my own land, and by treachery; never did I expect that. You two are here, are you; then at least something has gone as it should.'

Brannock had a great deal to say to him, but Eilian took no notice of that. 'Mennor,' she said, 'they don't listen to us.'

'They will now,' said Mennor roughly. 'If they'd like to ignore me, there's something behind me that's past ignoring. Go and fetch them out.'

'*Fetch?*' said Brannock, blenching at the thought.

'Yes, fetch.'

'I will,' said Eilian, and was off.

Brannock let her go; he was sure she did not need his help. 'Mennor,' he said, 'it was you as well as Eilian that Ansgar was hunting?'

'I know no Ansgar,' said Mennor. 'Petrock and Illtud were enough for me; combined of course with your father and Eilian's. You've heard about that, I take it.'

'Yes. Conan too?'

'I don't know about Conan. Your mother sent me warning when Petrock reappeared, and she and Aeronwy and Ingaret rode with me to Eastmark. She didn't believe that poor fool Rhodri had his heart in the plot, she thought Iorwenna would have talked some sense into him. But she'd bargained without Illtud.'

'Mother did!' said Brannock, cheered. It had not occurred to him that Ia would take her part in the politics. 'So what happened to them? And Eilian's brothers,' he added, ashamed that he had not thought of them earlier.

'That I don't know, because it became wiser for me to leave. But the last I heard, Iorwenna was washing her hands of Rhodri and demanding an escort to take the children south to her own family. And Illtud would not have interfered with that; *oh* no. *I* dealt with Illtud.'

'What did you do to him?'

'I cursed him,' Mennor said in simple pleasure. 'He was idiot enough to come within sight of me, and then to think he had power to get away from me. I cursed him living and dying, eating and drinking, waking and sleeping, and particularly I cursed him dreaming. Whoever else the invaders can bribe to their side, Illtud will be of no further use to them. Did they try to bribe you?'

'Yes, a man called Ansgar. But Mennor, what can be done now? It seems that the invaders are out over all the land, and in force.'

'Oh, they are in force all right, burning and killing wherever they go. And your father's men with them, because they're beginning to overrun the five kingdoms, and that means loot. There is only one thing to be done now. That's what I sent you for, and if I'd been wiser I'd have seen I was doing little good where I was and come myself. But that's behind us. Here I am, and there is work to be done. Do you see?'

He turned back south and pointed. The dolmen on the knoll stood solitary in the midday sun, and behind it stretched the barren slopes of the waste, and on the very farthest horizon, where the autumn mists became a purple haze, something moved; a ragged dark line slowly advanced towards them.

'Their main army,' Mennor said, watching it dispassionately. 'Advancing to outflank the five kingdoms; but probably, such is the nature of the land hereabouts, already a little confused about their direction. And here comes my colleagues of the Order.'

Brannock spared a moment from the situation to commend Eilian. He did not think that he could have brought the elders out in so short a time.

Maldwyn came first, with Teithi hovering anxiously at his side. The others followed two by two, in what Brannock supposed was some ceremonial order, except that after a few steps Scilti broke away from the others, looked anxiously south, and came trotting to Mennor's side. An elderly man holding up his robe to trot was not a very dignified sight; but suddenly Brannock preferred it to that of the solemn advance of the others.

Breathless, Scilti murmured to Mennor, 'Welcome – glad to see you safe – but on the skyline there – are my charms needed?'

'That would be useful,' Mennor said pleasantly. 'Nothing elaborate, Scilti, and certainly no mists or impenetrable marshes to frighten them away. Let them come, but not too fast, so that our preparations can be thorough.'

'Preparations?' Scilti said, and looked frightened. 'Mennor, what you propose—' He looked over his shoulder and saw Maldwyn near, and said hurriedly, 'Nothing elaborate, most certainly.' And gathering his robe round his knees he went to a distance and stood there, diligently murmuring. The dolmen melted into

116

two stag-headed oaks, and around it grew up a scrub of sapling oaks and fern and bramble.

Maldwyn came to a halt in front of Mennor and bowed to him, his hands folded into his sleeves. 'We are glad to see you safe,' he said, his voice in the open air thin and cold. 'We have welcomed your messengers and we thank you for your token. We have informed ourselves on the situation in the land.'

Without realizing it, Brannock had already decided that Maldwyn did not like Mennor. He saw now that Mennor was faintly scornful of Maldwyn. Seeing it clearly like this, he found it almost the most frightening thing that had yet happened. All his life he had been dimly aware that Mennor's authority was even greater than his father's; sent on this errand, he had taken it that, if he could only complete it, the power of the elders would mend all their troubles. And now here he and Eilian were, successfully having summoned the final help – and was it after all final? He looked around for Eilian; and saw her standing watching behind the line of elders, with Pangur riding her shoulder. Comfort or reinforcement?

Mennor bowed, not very deeply, to Maldwyn. 'I thank you for your welcome. I add to your knowledge of the situation that the enemy army is two miles away to the south.'

'Yes,' said Maldwyn, not looking at it, 'it is visible. We know that the two major kingdoms of the seven have joined it. We have been taking counsel as to our wisest course now.'

Mennor said, 'There is only one possible course.'

'Quite,' said Maldwyn thinly. 'I will myself talk to the leaders of this invasion.'

Brannock had thought himself not as brave as Eilian in speaking out in front of the elders. He found now that he was wrong. He burst out, 'No, never!'

Maldwyn turned his emotionless look on him and said, 'I do not believe that the kings now in alliance with the invaders will be able to obtain good terms for their people. I think I must do that.'

'Terms!' said Brannock, choking with fury.

'Terms!' Mennor echoed him, as if the word were a curse. 'Maldwyn, you're a coward. We are fighting them still. And we have one weapon that will defeat them finally.'

Maldwyn said, 'Yes. It will destroy them. What else will it destroy with them?'

'This is our land,' said Mennor. 'I vote for that final weapon. Who will vote with me?'

He swung on the line of the elders. They shuffled, muttered among themselves, looked wrung; but did not move. Brannock saw that it was not the question of the final weapon that stopped them; it was just that they were more in awe of Maldwyn than of Mennor. He said, 'I speak for Waymark.'

Eilian had appeared at his side. 'And I for Eastmark,' she said. She spoke almost offhandedly; she knew that it made no difference.

Maldwyn smiled at Mennor; and Brannock saw again that it was not the question of the final weapon that moved him, but his dislike of Mennor. 'This would seem to be a good moment,' he said. 'The leaders of the invasion are doubtless with that force now advancing upon us, and we can open negotiations at once.' He looked sidelong at Brannock. 'We are very skilled negotiators, king's son. How else do you think our Order has survived the countless peoples who have lived in this land? Scilti!'

Scilti came anxiously back.

'Arrange us something demanding respect, please;

a wall of mist rent by lightnings would be appropriate. I take it you will not be with us, Mennor? Nor the two young messengers? Well, don't worry yourselves for Waymark and Eastmark; we will see that they are treated kindly. You are ready, Scilti?'

The wall of mist came up nicely, creeping along the ground level with the stag-headed oaks and then rolling upwards into the sky. The stag-headed oaks, unwanted, became the dolmen again. Just as the mist thickened, the first of the enemy force appeared on the knoll, toiling up the slope; it was possible to watch their line break in confusion as they saw the mist. Scilti, murmuring, nodded to Maldwyn, and Maldwyn nodded to the line of elders. In solemn procession they marched into the mist, and it parted in front of them and reformed behind them. Scilti stayed where he was.

Mennor said roughly, 'Get on with you, Scilti, or Maldwyn will curse you.'

'I know,' Scilti said simply, 'but I don't agree with him.'

Eilian dug Brannock in the ribs and jerked her head backwards. He turned and saw Teithi standing awkwardly behind them. Honestly upset, he said to Mennor, 'Teithi's only a student, he'll get into trouble; let him go.'

'He isn't keeping me,' said Teithi. 'I just stayed.'

Scilti murmured again, and the mist advanced and closed into a tight circle around them. 'I don't know if that's any help, but no one can see or hear us. Can you do anything, Mennor?'

'Well,' said Mennor; he took some deep breaths and held each wrist in turn, exercising his fingers; 'we can try.'

Eilian said, 'I can do women's charms, and Brannock has the favour of the land.'

Teithi said, 'I don't think I can do anything but what you tell me.'

'I am good for nothing but illusions,' said Scilti, shaking his head.

Mennor said, 'This is a charm above all charms, and one which needs much strength to set it. Between us I don't believe that we have that strength. But what I shall try to summon is a power of the land, and I think we may succeed because the land itself is already uneasy. It is invaded; it is outraged. I think it will not need much to call the land to avenge itself.'

Eilian's mouth opened in astonishment. '*That*? Oh – well. Yes, I see; all right.'

Scilti said, 'It will be bad, of course. But then it's bad now. All right, Mennor.'

Teithi said, 'You will need wood,' and went away.

Brannock, with nothing to say, looked helplessly at Mennor.

'Stay with us,' said Mennor. 'It is the land we call. You will feel what is needed. Eilian, can you light the fire for me?'

'This is all wrong,' said Eilian. 'The wrong time of day, the wrong time of the moon. Scilti, where is a stone?'

The mist opened in front of her to show the threshold stone of the hall.

'Brannock, find me twigs.'

Brannock swept them up from the grass. When he put them on the stone, it tingled to him. He said to her, 'The land feels something. Go on.'

Eilian sank to her knees in front of the threshold stone. She undid the knot of her belt and shook her hair free. Teithi appeared with an armful of small wood and knelt behind her. She wrung her fingers and with a deep breath began to murmur.

'You are lying in darkness,' said Eilian. 'A friendly woman knocks at your door. Come out and greet her. There are friends here. Come out – and – be – welcomed!' She cupped her hands around the twigs on the stone. When she took them away the flame sprang up fiercely. She wiped her wet forehead with her arm, saying, 'Teithi!'

Teithi fed the fire, murmuring to it.

Brannock stood helpless, watching. The flames sprang higher, and he suddenly understood what was needed. He stripped off his arm-rings and his torque and threw them into the flames. The flames ate them as if they had been bark. Teithi, diffident, threw in his wallet and an amulet he took from his neck, and put on more logs. Scilti came forward and threw in a great armful that looked like tablets of runes. The fire roared up above their head. Eilian, still on her knees in front of it, threw in her brooch, her arm-rings, her girdle, and slashed at her hair and threw in a long lock, which crisped and flew upwards as an eddy of the smoke.

'Mennor,' said Scilti, his old voice cracking, 'quickly. I can't hold the mist against this.'

Mennor came forward to the fire. He was murmuring rapidly under his breath. He stripped off his thumb-rings and threw them in, saying, 'We invite to the need of the land the horses of the Hunter.' He threw in his wallet. 'We invite to the need of the land the hounds of the Hunter.' He threw in his belt and knife-sheath. 'We invite to our need the Hunter himself.' He took his knife and slashed his palm to the bone and threw the knife into the fire. 'We have here prey for the Hunter.'

The fire leapt to the skies and died. The mist began to shred away.

Now that the mist was gone, they could hear men talking outside the dolmen. It was quiet friendly talk, with a laugh now and again. It was evening already, clear and calm, with a slip of new moon lying on its back on the far hills.

Scilti said in a tired voice, 'I had better hide us.'

'Wait,' said Mennor.

Faintly over the hills came a sound so familiar that Brannock looked into the sky, expecting to see a skein of geese high above. But there were no geese in the sky. The noise grew upon them until it was the yell of hounds running a line, and over the hills like a hailstorm breaking came the red-eared hounds of the Hunter, and the red-eyed horses of the Hunter, and the antlered Hunter himself. And behind the Hunter rode the Wild Hunt of the land, yelling with fleshless lips.

The armed enemy turned and fled, and the Wild Hunt swept over the land.

Fifteen

Brannock understood, almost before the Wild Hunt
had made its first pass, what Maldwyn had meant. He
knew when he saw Eilian struggle to hold Pangur, and
Pangur rake his claws across her face and leap to
freedom. He knew when he tried to run clear with
Goldeneye in his arms, and found Teithi's body across
his way. The Wild Hunt may be invoked, but not controlled; once the Hunt is up, its prey is everything in
its path.

He shouted for Eilian, and thought he heard a faint
answer, and then the Hunt swept down on its second
pass. It struck with neither blade nor tooth; its
weapons were darkness and mindless panic and a
terrible tearing wind that picked him up and flung him
down and picked him up again before he had stopped
rolling. He lost Goldeneye, he lost all sense of what or
where he was, he stopped his ears and flattened
himself to the ground in terror against the third
passing of the Wild Hunt.

He wandered, after that, for a long stupid time in
noisy darkness. There were trees that he fell against,
and rocks that he sprawled clumsily over, and once he
heard a voice moaning, but never found out who it
was, or where. In the end he lost the wish to pick
himself up and stayed where he had fallen, huddled

in a tangle of tree-roots, jerked awake, whenever his eyes closed, by the panic fear of the Wild Hunt.

Was it still dark, or again dark, when Goldeneye crawled whimpering to his side? They lay shivering, not daring to move. It was many hours before thirst drove them to venture out.

The forest they were in was strange to him. The trees were sparse but enormous, red-trunked, rising bare to the crown of deep glossy green; the ground below them was soft with shed needles. There was no water, and the only life a small weasel-like animal that screamed hatred at them from the tree-tops.

As once before, the only direction they had was downhill. It was two days before they dragged themselves over a bank and found a stream below. Its edges were fringed with fine ice; it seemed that winter was come. They never did find food, but a day after this came out of the forest under a green evening sky and saw the entrance dolmen very black against the light. The lintel-stone had fallen and the other two were broken. They passed them on their right and looked into the centre of Caerdroia.

The smooth turf was rutted and scarred by bramble and nettle. The stone circle was broken, only two of the lintel stones still in place and many of the uprights overthrown. He walked to the threshold stone, which was splintered across, and sat on a fallen block and looked at Goldeneye. He was thin and scarred, his coat torn and matted with burrs. He looked down at himself and thought that he must look much the same; and then a disgust of such self-pity came over him.

He got to his feet and cuffed Goldeneye up. 'Stop being sorry for yourself. Hunt for our supper while I make camp.'

He turned and saw Maldwyn looking out of the splintered door of the hall.

'Our hospitality,' he said, 'is not what it was, but you are welcome.'

'Thank you,' said Brannock, and went in. The hall was a ruin, but an inhabitable ruin, with a reasonable amount of roof and a good fire going. 'Goldeneye,' he said, 'a coney at least for our hosts, please.' Goldeneye obediently trotted off. Brannock looked round the company and said, 'I am glad to see so many of you.'

Maldwyn had gone back to his high chair; its rich coverings had gone, and so had most of the treasures that had once been there. There were five elders and three servants, all men. The servants, though without energy, were mixing and cooking bread cakes, but the elders were doing nothing. One of the servants brought him a drink and put a stool for him beside Maldwyn. He drank, and since no one had anything to say surveyed the hall. 'The frame is still sound,' he said, 'and it should be easy enough to mend the roof.'

The servant who had brought his drink looked at him; but that was all. After a time Goldeneye trotted in carrying a coney, and it was the same servant, a short black-haired man with a great breadth of chest, who took it from him and started preparing it. Brannock went to the fire to see that Goldeneye was given his share, and this man said irritably, 'I know how to feed a hunting dog.'

'What's your name?'

'Huw, sir.'

'Have you carpentry tools we could use on the roof?'

Huw thought briefly and said, 'There's no knowing what's buried in all that rubble. I'll have a look in the morning.' He had a cauldron over the fire, and put in the coney to stew with roots and herbs. It was a sparse meal, but there was plenty of bread, and it brought a little life into the elders; there was quite an argument about the size of the portions of meat. When they had finished Huw brought out a jug of wine, and murmured to Brannock as he served him, 'There are jobs more urgent than the roof.'

'Tomorrow, then. What happened to the maids?'

'They said their families would need them in the troubles, and left.'

'You didn't see Eilian?'

'The red-haired one? I'm sorry, no.'

One of the elders pottered over to have his cup filled again, and it was Scilti. He looked very old, and was drowsy and forgetful. Brannock complimented him on the quality of his illusion around the hall, but he shook his head. 'I'm losing touch with unreality,' he said sadly. 'In my younger days I could have made a ruined hall look like a palace or a hovel. Now it's all I can do to make it look like a ruined stone circle.'

'It isn't a ruined hall,' said Brannock, and nodded to Huw that he would refill Maldwyn's cup himself. Maldwyn too looked older, but not sleepy; rather, too proud to be anything but faintly scornful. Since scorn was not likely to be helpful, Brannock changed his mind about speaking of the state of the hall, and said instead, 'Sir, I would like news of my cousin Eilian. Or of her cat Pangur or her horse the Bach Bychan.'

Maldwyn shook his head.

Well, he had expected that. If Eilian had been there, they would not have been sitting slumbrous among ruins. And he would have been really worried if Pangur or the Bychan had been here without her.

'Teithi,' he said soberly, 'I know about. But Mennor?'

126

Maldwyn turned his eyes on him. 'No, Brannock. You know that too. It was Mennor's blood on the knife that brought the Wild Hunt.'

Huw made up the fire for the night, and went off into a dark corner and brought out a blanket for Brannock. Goldeneye came to share it with him, and a wizened elder woke up and accused Huw of giving him the last bread-cake. Huw said crisply, 'The dog provided your meat. Goodnight, reverend sirs.'

They slept in the warmth of the fire.

Brannock was up early in the morning, only just after Huw. He helped him make up the fire, and noted with pleasure that there was a good store of dry wood. There was a sharp white frost on the grass. He said privately to Huw, 'My dog can't hunt for so many. Have you no stores of food?'

'That's what needs doing before the roof,' Huw said crossly. 'Of course there are stores, if one could get at them. There's a grain-pit full, and the smoke-room with meat and fish, and roots stored to blanch. But they're all outside where everything's down, and I've cleared the small stuff but the beams are too much for one, and they won't stir a hand to help themselves.'

'They will,' said Brannock.

But they did not get to the food-stores all at once, because the winter snows came down on them, and first they had to stop them filling the hall. Brannock grew savage with those elders who refused to climb on scaffolding and hammer in pegs in a blizzard. He told them what he thought of them, several times and in scalding detail, and then gave up and made them rip down the few planks they had managed to get up, so that he could drive them instead into building a partition across the weather-tight part of the hall. This was easier, since it did not need scaffolding, and Scilti

127

became quite brisk. Brannock never quite succeeded in setting Maldwyn to carpentry, but by being rigidly courteous he did persuade him to superintend the others. While Brannock bullied the elders, Huw cursed the remaining servants until they began to think usefully. One of them turned out to know about rabbit-wiring, so that Goldeneye did not have to be sent out so often to hunt. The other, after several weeks of unexplained melancholy, erupted into the hall one evening, shouting, 'It didn't matter that we'd quarrelled!', and dragged in a black-haired girl carrying a bundle. Her name was Ide; she said composedly that a silly quarrel had had nothing to do with her leaving; she had had to see her old father settled after the troubles; now she had come back to look after her reverend gentlemen, providing – with a searing glance – that this fool Tegid would let her go about her business and start cleaning this disgusting hall. It had got rather dirty with their carpentry, and after a couple of hours she had them all terrorized, including Brannock. She was so scathing about his habit of not clearing his adze-chippings after him that it was a whole day before he took her aside and asked, 'Ide, what happened to Eilian?'

'The red-haired one?' said Ide, stooping to brush up the cinders. 'You've lost her again? That's your carelessness. Had she anyone to look after?'

'Not here. She had a horse and a cat.'

'Hm,' said Ide, and with a thumb-nail scratched at a stain on his tunic. 'The horse I can't say about, but when you go round the traps you might get news of the cat. Anyone knows that cats don't travel far. And do I have to ask day after day to have the bath-house repaired? All your clothes are disgusting, and what can I do about it when the bath-house is a ruin?'

So once again the roof had to wait, while they rebuilt the bath-house.

Brannock took her advice, and kept a sharp look-out when he went round the rabbit-wires. The snow was lying thickly, and there was, now and again, a line of two pairs of five pads. He followed it, and was rewarded by two green eyes and a snarl from a high branch. He skinned and gutted a coney there, talking quietly about Eilian, and in the morning the snow was clean and the five-pad tracks thick around it. He did it again, and then again, each time nearer to the hall. Then he spoke to Ide about it, and was told that he was cruel to dumb animals and had better leave it to her. After that there was a second dish beside Goldeneye's each evening, and Pangur prowled the hall as by right.

With the thaw came Ide's younger sister Olwen, who after much fierce whispering disappeared for a night and came back with two brothers and a cousin, and, surprisingly, a stiff-jointed elder called Eifion, whom they had found wandering and sheltered for the winter. He, not knowing how much they had rebuilt, spoke contemptuously of the state of the hall, and irritated everyone into further efforts. To Brannock's astonishment, the roof was positively repaired, and the winter partition dismantled. The kitchen and bath-house were in use, and the supply of food good. Brannock talked long with Ide and Olwen and their menfolk about what had happened in the land since he and Eilian had left their homes. It was in a bad way, they told him. The invaders had gone through much of it with fire and sword, and had not much troubled, it seemed to him, to spare the lives and goods of their allies of Waymark and Eastmark; the coming of the Wild

129

Hunt had put a stop to that, but – they shook their heads.

'Well, Brannock boy, you were there; you know what the Hunt does to men.'

Yes, he knew. One evening on the edge of spring he took his stool after supper and sat by Maldwyn's side.

'I think I have done all that I can here,' he said.

Maldwyn looked at him in his still and distant way and said, 'You want to leave us.'

'Yes. There must be a great deal to be done elsewhere.'

'Yes. The invaders were defeated, but the people had to pay for it.'

'As Mennor paid. Will you tell me, please, how to find the way out of Caerdroia?'

Maldwyn regarded him thoughtfully. 'You ask me that? You who own the bob?'

'Yes,' said Brannock, who had been thinking about it. 'I am the intruder here, even if it was by the favour of the land. It will be proper for me to leave by your way.'

'Call Tegid,' said Maldwyn.

He spoke to him privately and briefly. Tegid gave Brannock a gloomy look and went away. When they made the fire up for the night, Huw said in Brannock's ear, 'Look, you don't want to take it unkindly. It was the repairs, see; they wanted you to stay till they were done. But don't worry, they won't hinder you now that spring's here.'

In the middle of next morning Tegid stalked into the hall, gave Brannock another look, and spoke to Maldwyn. Maldwyn crooked a finger for Brannock.

'To find your way out of Caerdroia,' he said, 'you need only to have found your way in. Ride westward. You will find the Bach Bychan at the door. Goodbye,

Brannock. Thank you for your work this long time.'

Brannock opened his mouth to say a great deal; not least about the Bach Bychan, because he had found much comfort in the thought that he had been with Eilian. But he shut it again. 'Goodbye, Maldwyn,' he said, 'and thank you for your hospitality.'

'Perhaps we owe you one word of warning,' said Maldwyn. 'You ride home. Remember then that the Wild Hunt has harrowed the land, as well as the easterners. And where the Wild Hunt has passed things are liable to be changed.'

'Changed how?'

'You will discover soon enough.'

Sixteen

He would not have a word said against the Bychan, but he had forgotten how very small he was. Huw had put up a fat food-bag, and Ide had woven him an osier-basket into which she stuffed a terribly-swearing Pangur, and once he was mounted, with the bag on his shoulder and the basket balanced in front of him, he would not have been surprised to find his feet scraping the ground.

Huw said, 'Now don't you fret yourself about the Bychan. His legs are short but his back and heart are strong. Good speed on your way, Brannock boy, and good news at the end of it.' Ide gave him instructions on how to feed his animals, and conveyed her immovable belief that he would not do it properly. Neither of them spoke of his ever returning.

He turned the Bychan's head to the west. He had snared coneys in these low hills with their stretches of scrub woodland, hardly remembering that some-where in them must lie the last circles of the troy, those circles which only Eilian and Pangur had travelled. It would be interesting, he thought now, to see the way she had come; though she had surely said something about valleys too steep for riding? For some reason that escaped him (there had been so much on his mind lately), she had never told him much about the last stages of her lonely journey.

There was no sign of the land's becoming broken.

The birch woods grew thicker, and with the small leaves of the beginning of spring were in a glow of green above their dark boles. After a couple of miles he reined in in uncertainty. This shifting light was not the dazzle of spring; it had become a mist, a queer rolling mist which at one moment was thick and grey and at the next shot through with gold. How was he to keep direction now? He looked round for Goldeneye, and found him at his stirrup, motionless, ears pricked and nose quivering at something that ran silently across their path from out of the mist.

It was a great grey wolf, trotting low to the ground. It looked over its shoulder at them as it vanished among the trees, and the light caught its golden eyes. The Bychan turned his head placidly to watch it, and Goldeneye sat down and thumped his tail.

Understanding, if only dimly, Brannock lifted his hand to it and called, 'Goodbye!' He loosed the rein and the Bychan and Goldeneye trotted on undirected. After that he kept a watch above, waiting for gaps in the mist. Presently he saw a far-distant speck; it fell through the high airs, checked, circled on barred wings and wide tail, and closed its wings and fell like a stone towards him. It swept over them on a five-foot span of pinions, a buzzard, its golden beak gaping, and swung up into the sky and hovered as the mist rolled over them.

'Goodbye, goodbye!' said Brannock. He rode soberly on, wondering how he would find the world now that he had left Caerdroia for ever. When he reckoned that they had crossed seven miles, he dismounted beside a small stream to rest the Bychan, and after a time, as on any fine spring morning, the mist dispersed and the sun shone, and looking back he saw behind them nothing but a stretch of brown moorland with some birch spinneys shining with the first leaves of spring.

Since Eilian's village was the nearer, in the afternoon he gave the Bychan his head, and he turned a point or two south in a comfortingly confident way. Presently he came across a hut, a rather pathetic one of turves and branches, but in a good place beside a pool, where a tired young woman was struggling to make a fire burn while she nursed a baby and tried to stop two little ones falling in the pool. He built up the fire for her, and with some broken branches improvised a jack to hold her cauldron over it, while she explained that her husband was busy breaking a new patch of land. When he pulled a sour face at the tumbledown hut she fired up and told him not to criticize a man who was working to provide for his family; so that when the husband came home at sundown he found Brannock half-way through firming the worst of the turf walls, and plenty in the cauldron thanks to Goldeneye. The two older children had to be stopped overfeeding Goldeneye, but Pangur had already taught them not to worry him when he wanted to sleep.

The husband, unlike his wife, was big and yellow-headed, and at first seemed surly; but in fact he was only tired to the bone, and once revived by a good meat meal was cheerfully full of plans. He was breaking a fine piece of land, whose harvest would keep them through the winter, and these parts, as his guest's excellent dog had shown, were full of game, once he could find the time to go after it. Next year he would break a fresh field, and by the time the boys were old enough to help he reckoned to have a flourishing holding. Seed-corn he had got by helping a neighbour three miles south, and he had seeds too for a plot round the hut. So next day Brannock finished shoring up the hut and dug a plot for the seeds, and they did their best to persuade him to stay in partnership.

'I'm sorry,' he said, 'but I have kin I must find farther west. You never heard news of one Eilian, a red-haired girl?'

They wanted to know of what family she was, and he said reluctantly, 'Rhodri's daughter,' because he did not know how Rhodri was regarded these days. But the husband looked vaguely at his wife, and both shook their heads.

'No, we don't know that family. But we had to move in the troubles that autumn, like most people, and we haven't had the time to travel abroad.'

'Where did you come from?'

The husband waved his hand to the east, and the wife said laughing, 'That was how we met! I lost my people in the troubles – I'm from farther north, I expect you can hear that in the way I talk – and I found him lying hurt not far from here, and when I'd got him better we found this good place and settled.'

Brannock looked sidelong at the children. The two elder might have been twins, but surely at least two years old? He stayed one more day, because he saw a good way of building a chimney on to the hut, and left them with regrets early the next morning. The husband shook his hand heartily and said, 'You'll be a welcome guest at any time.' The wife said, 'Bring Eilian to see us.'

This morning the Bach Bychan went between south-west and south steadily, and Pangur lay in the osier-basket without complaint. Around sunset of a clear spring day they came over the hill and saw a village street below them.

* * *

The truth was that Brannock had not noticed much about Eilian's village except Rhodri's hall, and that was gone, and some little garden plots covered the spot where he thought it had been. The street now looked very much like any other street at that time of day, with the children playing games and stopping to stare at the stranger; but the Bychan came to a halt, and Pangur took one leap from the basket and was gone. Brannock dismounted and slapped off the worst of the dust, and wondered if any of the children remembered him. But then he did not look very much like the old Brannock king's son; no torque, no arm-rings, no golden brooch to hold his cloak in the proper folds. He wore the much more useful hooded tunic of the people, his cloak was his blanket, and he had long ago taken a knife to his hair and cut it short to the nape. He was thinking of asking for Iorwenna when a woman came out of the biggest hut and said, 'Who are you, stranger?' She was his sister Ingaret.

He let her look at him, waiting for her to shriek in recognition and throw herself on him; but instead she turned and called into the hut. 'If you need shelter for the night,' she said, 'speak to my husband.'

He had started to laugh at her when her husband came out of the hut. He was Ansgar.

He greeted Brannock kindly. 'You're travelling west? Come in and welcome. There's a stall for your horse over there, and bring in your dog too. We can't give you ale to drink, like everyone else we've had some difficult seasons, but our water's good and we can give you supper and a bed. What, a coney?' (for Brannock had had Goldeneye see to it that they did not come empty-handed). 'Thank you, that's kind. We're too busy with the ploughing to hunt just now.'

He was not very much like the splendid figure by the dolmen of Caerdroia. Like Brannock, he wore working clothes without ornaments, and when he sat down with a sigh inside the hut it was with the sigh of a man was has worked hard all day. There was, Brannock noted dumbly, a baby in the cradle by the fire.

'Have you news?' Ansgar asked when Ingaret had brought them water and gone back to her cooking. 'How are things to the east?'

Brannock said slowly, 'I was working some days with a family there, a plot by a stream, breaking new ground.'

Ansgar nodded. 'One of my men. Yes, he'll do well there, it's good land. You were working for him? I should tell you in all friendliness, we've nothing to spare here, even for an able-bodied man like yourself. You won't take it amiss, I hope. You know how things are since the troubles.'

'Yes,' said Brannock, 'yes. I was hoping only for news. I come from – from farther west, but I knew this kingd – land once. I would be glad to hear about it.'

'Well,' said Ansgar, stretching his legs comfortably, 'you've seen my wife, she's a local girl, from the next village along. That was pretty well destroyed in the troubles and her father killed, so she and her mother moved in with some kin here. Her mother lives two miles down the road, with the other girl – she'll be marrying this spring too. Another reason we can't be as hospitable as we'd like; we have to help them a good deal, my brother Conan got a leg-wound in the troubles and doesn't get about very well yet.'

'And Iorwenna and Rhodri?'

'Oh, Rhodri.' Ansgar smiled broadly. 'I shouldn't

137

laugh at my own uncle, but he really did make himself unpopular. Hardly a roof left intact in the village, and all he would talk about was having his hall rebuilt. We were thankful for aunt Iorwenna, who took him and the boys off south, where there's another branch of the family.'

'And are you king here,' Brannock asked, 'or is it Conan?'

'Oh, I suppose Conan,' Ansgar said lazily. 'He has the brains of the family, but then he's not much use yet at the work. We settle things between us when we have to, but on the whole we're too busy to worry about such things yet.'

'And in the village to the west,' Brannock asked after a pause, 'is that quite deserted?'

'Oh quite,' Ansgar said cheerfully. 'Everyone left there moved down here, for the neighbourliness.' He sent a sharp look in Brannock's direction, but to Brannock it seemed to slide oddly away from him. 'Have you a place of your own, or are you looking to settle? There's not a roof left, you know.'

The baby woke and cried, and Ingaret left the fire to pick him up. 'Supper in a moment,' she said, and sat down beside them. 'Big and yellow-headed,' she said thoughtfully, though looking not at Brannock but at the baby. 'You must be of my husband's people from the east.'

Astounded, Brannock said, 'I was born – not very far from here.'

'Ah!' said Ansgar approvingly, 'then you have eastern blood in you. Ingaret won't believe me, but our family records go back I don't know how many generations to an earlier Ansgar who also came west overseas and settled here. He was thought the disgrace of the family, because their way in those days

138

was to raid and run. Sheer piracy, of course. But he liked it and married and settled, and sent word back that he was doing well in a good land.' He laughed and clapped Brannock on the shoulder. 'So it's all in the family, perhaps!'

'And the latest Ansgar,' said Ingaret, jumping the baby on her knee, 'will inherit it.'

'I hope he will do well,' said Brannock, rising. 'And thank you for the rest, but I must be going. My good wishes to – to all the family.'

They protested, and tried to give him back the coney, but he took Goldeneye and the Bach Bychan and rode westwards.

Well, it was hard to know what to make of all that.

He tried feeling outraged, and he tried feeling angry, and neither seemed to fit him. Then he tried feeling sorry for himself, and found instead that he was enormously amused. All in the family, was it now? No, there was nothing else to do but to laugh, long and silently.

He rode two miles until he came to the hut where his mother and Conan and Aeronwy were living. It looked prosperous enough, with a good wood-pile and a cow-shed, though a small one; but surely Conan could have mended the fence, even if he did go lame? The truth was that Conan had always been lazy. He went quietly by, left Goldeneye and the Bychan a quarter of a mile up the road, and made his way through the trees to the back of the hut. As he had thought – plenty of stakes there to make the fence good! He stood watching in the dusk until he saw his mother come out and go into the cow-shed, and from there he heard her voice – scolding Aeronwy, at a guess. She looked brisk and busy. And there was

Conan, not even having to use a stick, looking out of the door at the weather, and going in again.

He searched around the wood-pile until he found a handy small log that would serve as a mallet, shouldered some stakes, and stole to the gap in the fence. The ground was soft, and the stakes went in with very little noise from the hammering. He heeled in the earth around them, pulled some strands of ivy (why hadn't Conan cleared it away?) and twined them in and out of the stakes, laughing inwardly until he shook. The door of the hut opened again, and he heard Conan calling, and Aeronwy answering from the cow-shed. Conan came out with a rush, hardly limping at all, shouting, 'Who is it, who's there?' He burst out laughing, 'Ho ho ho!', and skipped off up the road, leaving them to wonder.

He had meant to camp as soon as he was clear of the village, but a good white moon got up, and the Bychan went clopping sturdily on without objections, and he thought that he could be home before morning.

Not a roof left there, his brother-in-law had said. Well, that was all right; he was good with roofs. There would be timber and tools enough if he ferreted among the ruins, and who knew better than he where the good land was? He would build a hut and clear a plot; and then he would find Eilian.

He rode through the small wood where the best nuts would be in the autumn, and saw the stone circle standing very black in the moonlight. It was broken, as he had expected. He passed it on his right hand and rode to the edge of the rise to look lovingly down on his lost village.

Except that it was not lost.

The king's hall had gone, the cultivated fields and

byres had gone, the village street had gone. But around the well was a tiny cluster of four huts and one half-built, with a feather of smoke rising to shine in the moonlight.

He sat there for a long time, with Goldeneye beside the Bychan, and for the first time he was uncertain. Others had come to his village before him, homeless folk from other parts who had built their huts from the ruins. So what was he to do now?

Goldeneye's nose nudged his foot. He turned his head and saw two green eyes gleam at him from between the broken stones.

He dismounted and led the Bach Bychan into the stone circle. Eilian was waiting for him with Pangur on her shoulder.

'You were a long time coming,' she said.

She had a fire going in a sheltered place between two fallen stones, and she toasted dried meat on bread-cakes while they talked under the white moon.

'You aren't living here?'

'No, I was waiting for you. I've got a hut in the woods over there, but when Pangur arrived tonight I thought I'd find you here.'

'I'm sorry I was so long. I came as soon as I could, but there was so much to be done first. How long was it, do you think? It seemed to me only one winter.'

'Oh no, more than that, I'm sure. Did you stay in Caerdroia? Time goes slowly there, I think. Or is it quickly?'

'Yes, I had to stay, they needed looking after. For elders, you know, they are amazingly helpless. And then Pangur and the Bychan were there, though I didn't find them at once. Where were you?'

'Oh, I couldn't tell you. I got blown away by the Wild Hunt. That's the worst of being little, you blow away so easily. Then I fell in with a lot of people running from the Hunt. I think they were easterners but I was never certain. They were quite friendly, but so helpless. I did some charms to help them when the Hunt had passed.'

'What kind of charms?'

'Fire-making and weather, mostly. There were quite a lot of us in the end, and some of them weren't easterners because they insisted on going back north where they'd come from. Do you know, we passed the Stonesmiths' House once, and I went in to look for Ambrosianus, but he wasn't there. At least, I don't think he was. Something sighed and flickered once or twice, but when I looked directly there was nothing there.'

'I was never really sure how much he was there. Did you see the gate and the steps?'

'Yes, I looked specially, but there wasn't even the hedge. I'll tell you who was there, though. Lysis.'

'Who?'

'You remember, his hunting bitch that he missed so much. I wanted to go into what was left of the villa to look for Niall and his wife, but I couldn't, because she kept appearing on the terrace and snarling at me. I don't wonder he missed her, she was a splendid dog. So you don't have to worry about breaking your promise to send him puppies.'

'I'm glad of that. Could the others see the villa?'

'I don't think so, but they said it was a frightening place and wouldn't go near it. They didn't see the troy either, but then I don't think I did; we just went any way that seemed easy. I suppose because they weren't looking for it.'

142

'They weren't. You'd found it. Maldwyn said that to find your way out of the troy you need only to have found your way in. So what did you do then?'

'I can't remember it all. I went north with some of them for a time, because the weather was bad and we thought we should stay together. There were villages up there that weren't in a bad state, because the easterners hadn't got so far; there hadn't been any burning and killing, just the Wild Hunt that made them all too frightened to do much. Well, there was always something that needed doing, sometimes with charms but mostly with a little good sense. I never really knew who the people were, our own or the invaders. It didn't seem to matter really, they were all in the same trouble.'

'Ansgar said – oh, I didn't tell you, he's married my sister – he said that there were some of his people living here long ago.'

'Well, you remember what Ambrosianus told us. So you saw your family?'

'Didn't you see yours?'

'No. I don't want to.'

She wore her unforgiving face. If Ansgar could afford to laugh a little at Rhodri, Brannock reflected, so could she; but not yet. He said peaceably, 'Your mother and brothers are all right; they've gone south. . . . But Eilian – none of them knew me; not even my sister.'

'Well—' said Eilian, and picked up Pangur and stroked him, 'I did go and look at my village; just a look. And the men working in the fields were strangers, so I thought I might ask them for news. But I don't think they saw me properly.'

'How was that?'

'They must have come from a poor thin land,

because they were sowing too thick, so I told them how to do it properly for this land. But what they did was to discuss it among themselves and decide that they could sow thinner. And when I asked them questions they only talked among themselves, and they didn't look at me.'

'I know,' said Brannock, and remembered Ansgar, sitting at his ease, talking cheerfully, but with his eyes looking anywhere but directly at Brannock. 'I think it must be because we were in Caerdroia.'

'Yes; I thought that too. Time was different there, wasn't it? I thought we'd only been away one winter, but it must have been more. It could be as much as—'

'Seven years.'

'Yes. Have we become part of the land?'

'Well, we were that before.'

'Yes. And now the land has taken the invaders to itself—'

'And Ansgar and Ingaret have a baby—'

'And we can't tell which are the invaders and which are our own people . . . Well,' said Eilian practically, 'then it can't matter, can it? And we have Pangur and Goldeneye and the Bach Bychan, and if the people who have settled down there can't see us, they can see what we do, and they're going to need help, like all the rest of them since we left Caerdroia.'

'Yes, we shall be busy,' said Brannock. 'And I forgot to tell you, I staked my lazy brother's fence on the way here. I must go back in a day or two and see that he's put some good osier in place of my ivy. And if the he doesn't get down to some work, I'll – I'll get you to weather-charm him into the duck-pond.'